PRAISE FOR
THE LAST ISLAND

"Human nature and authority come face-to-face in Livaneli's unparalleled, creative novel. The author invites us to rethink the world we live in."
—Lenore Martin, Emmanuel College and Harvard University

"This haunting fable of a President's war against seagulls feels all the more relevant to our times in its absurdity and heartbreak. Livaneli has written a lucid account of a community's shattering alongside natural devastation. A wise and piercing book."
—Ayşegül Savaş, author of *White on White* and *Walking on the Ceiling*

"Urgent and allegorical, Livaneli is masterful in his depiction of how authoritarian power destroys a community's people and environment. *The Last Island* is a stunning novel that will stay with me for a long time."
—Mina Seçkin, author of *The Four Humors*

"With this novel Livaneli has entered through the grand gates of literature."

—Yashar Kemal, author of *Memed, My Hawk*

"This book is a recipe of what authoritarianism is made of. Some readers might start the reading thinking this is directed only at current politics in Turkey. However, it quickly emerges that it is about decades of power struggles, with a message that within this vicious circle there are no happy endings."

—Louis Fishman, author of *Jews and Palestinians in the Late Ottoman Era, 1908–1914: Claiming the Homeland*

"In this beautifully written book, Livaneli poetically recounts the story of how societies get corrupted by self-serving autocratic leaders. Livaneli's riveting *The Last Island* provides a much-needed and uplifting read for all in need of resilience and hope."

—Soner Cagaptay, author of *A Sultan in Autumn: Erdogan Faces Turkey's Uncontainable Forces*

THE LAST ISLAND

ALSO BY ZÜLFÜ LIVANELI

Disquiet

Serenade for Nadia

Bliss

THE
LAST
ISLAND

Zülfü Livaneli

Translated from the Turkish by Ayşe A. Şahin

OTHER PRESS

NEW YORK

Production editor: Yvonne E. Cárdenas
Text designer: Jennifer Daddio
This book was set in Cochin by
Alpha Design & Composition of Pittsfield, NH

1 3 5 7 9 10 8 6 4 2

Library of Congress Cataloging-in-Publication Data
Names: Livaneli, Zülfü, 1946- author. | Şahin, Ayşe A. (Ayşe Aydan),
1969- translator.
Title: The last island : a novel / Zülfü Livaneli ; translated from the
Turkish by Ayşe A. Şahin.
Other titles: Son ada. English
Description: New York : Other Press, 2022.
Identifiers: LCCN 2021058990 (print) | LCCN 2021058991 (ebook) |
ISBN 9781635422221 (paperback ; acid-free paper) |
ISBN 9781635422238 (ebook)
Subjects: LCGFT: Novels.
Classification: LCC PL248.L58 S6613 2022 (print) |
LCC PL248.L58 (ebook) | DDC 894/.3533—dc23/eng/20220304
LC record available at https://lccn.loc.gov/2021058990
LC ebook record available at https://lccn.loc.gov/2021058991

My blood still flows salty
Where the oysters slit my skin.

—ORHAN VELI

T HERE WAS A TIME when we were peacefully going about our lives in this paradise-on-earth, the one we had thought of as a well-kept secret. Until the day "He" showed up.

How to describe this paradise, even attempt to describe it, is simply beyond me. If I were to speak of this tiny island's pine forests, its cerulean sea as clear as nature's own aquarium, its alluring coves with their brightly colored fish that mesmerized us as we watched them, and its seagulls that always flew around us like white ghosts—this might be a scene that would amount to no more than a tourist postcard.

Far from any continent, it was a world unto itself, its night air releasing the delicate sweet scent of jasmine, cloaked in the same mild climate regardless of the season, it existed entirely independently with its forty houses nestled among the trees.

It was as if some sacred secret were hidden in the tranquil nature of the island. How could one begin to describe the morning's milky white mist above the sea, the early evening's light breeze licking your face, the whispering of the wind amid the cries of the seagulls, the scent of lavender? Or the spell cast each morning by the misty twin-island that would appear before us as though suspended from the sky while we were still rubbing the sleep from our eyes? Or the seagulls, diving in and out of the sea in their hunt for prey? Or the violet bougainvilleas that entwined our houses?

The fact is, it no longer even occurred to us how beautiful this life was. We'd grown so used to it that we were just going about our lives as usual, really. You don't think of the sea as being beautiful; nor do you think of a seagull alighting on a rock cliff in front of your house as being beautiful, when it's something you see every day. Nor of the way the branches of the trees meet and intertwine into a canopy as you walk along the dirt path running through a copse, nor of the quiet conversations amid the gardens, where the morning glories bloom like a sudden miracle, nor of the whispers of love that waft, almost inaudibly, from a house here and there. A person simply experiences them. But being neither a professional writer nor a good one, I've chosen to tell you about everything by means of a series of descriptions. In truth, it is my friend, the Writer, who should be telling you this story. But sadly for us all, his fate has made this impossible.

He was my closest friend on the island for years, and who knows what clever metaphors he could have worked into the text in telling you the story. So it's unfortunate that you have no choice but to learn of the horrifying events that befell the island and my friend from me. Bear with me, the common writer that I am, ignorant of all forms of modern novels and elaborate techniques of exposition.

The fact of the matter is, back then we didn't want any of this to get out. We would keep our island a jealously guarded secret, given that in our increasingly insane world, it hardly would have suited our interests for others to find out that a place like this even existed. We were the forty resident families of the island who somehow had been fortunate enough for it to have entered our lives.

We were living in peace, without anyone interfering in anyone else's business.

Having previously suffered considerable disappointment and deep sorrow, I deeply felt that the new friends that all of us had made on the island were precious beyond words, and I loved them genuinely. So much so that I nicknamed this place "Isle of Angels." Yes, we really were living on an isle of angels now. The only thing we wished for was to continue leading this life of peace.

As we had no television reception, the newspapers brought in by the weekly ferry were the only way we had of finding out about what was going on in the world. With eyes half-closed as we were about to doze off on the heels of a lunch taken with wine, we read the news on this untroubled little planet of ours, seeing reports that the insanity on that other planet was on the rise. But I must admit this news may as well have been about the space wars, for all we were concerned. It was all so remote to us.

We were mistaken, however, as we found out in the end. Far from being a separate planet, what we were was an island in the very belly of the insanity—a reality we failed to see even as the President settled on our island after having reluctantly concluded his term as the nation's head of state.

I should fill you in on some of this island's history. Years ago, when it was deserted, the island was bought by a wealthy businessman. In his old age, he built a magnificent country house, where he settled in with a staff of servants. He lived out the last years of his life far removed from the struggles of the world, spending his time fishing and napping in his hammock in the afternoons.

To relieve his boredom, he invited a few acquaintances to his home and encouraged them to build homes of their own. They came and built houses that were smaller than his, so he didn't ask them for any payment for the land. The houses were built of natural materials by the islanders, making use of the island's forests for the log cabin–style houses, so that only a bare minimum of construction materials needed to be shipped in from elsewhere. In time, as word spread among friends and acquaintances, the number of houses on the island reached forty. It was then that the wealthy man put a stop to further arrivals and to the construction of any more houses, to prevent any spoilage of the island's natural beauty, its serenity and its forests that shimmered with a thousand and one shades of green.

When this man passed away, he willed the house to his oldest son. Being something of an idler, the son preferred to spend his life on the island in leisure rather than assuming the more complex job of governing the island. In time, he came to forget, as did the other island residents, that the island actually belonged to his family, whom the islanders regarded as no different from anyone else—they just lived in a larger house.

We called him Number 1. It wasn't because he was the leader, or was particularly distinguished, or even that he had descended from the island's original owner, but because of an odd tradition around here: We tend to address folks by the number of their house.

My family's number is 36. My father found his way to this island rather late in the ownership sequence of the forty houses. Through invitations from some acquaintances, he managed to seize the opportunity, despite a history of prior personal disappointments, to grab the fourth-from-last house. As for my friend the Writer, though neither he nor his family owned a house here, he had a close friend who was a fan of his books and who let him use his house at a time when the Writer had been looking for a quiet place to write. He was Number 7. His was one of the first houses on the island, at the head of a dirt path that lined a shady tunnel woven by majestic trees.

The row of houses starts at the tip of the island where a ramshackle pier stands. A weekly ferry approaches it, but it's never able to touch the pier because that ferry is so enormous it has to be anchored offshore while small boats carry supplies to the island. From there, the houses are numbered 1, 2, 3, 4, and so on, in lockstep progression until they reach 40. Next to the pier there's a small grocery that meets all our needs, and a simple garden café run by the same man, which offers seafood and fresh fish on a daily basis. We simply call this old veteran "the grocer." This is because he has no number. He lives with his wife and their son, a young man, in the two-room annex behind the shop. He had arrived and settled on the island with his family years ago, and is now an inseparable part of it.

So I'm hoping at this point that I've provided the necessary information about the island before I start telling you the story. I hope I haven't left anything out! Rest assured, I would have liked to have given you an account of all this in a manner full of literary flair—more like a pro, that is. Yet, being an ordinary storyteller, I can't help telling the story in simple terms. All these hours at my notebook, I continually admonish myself: Do as modern writers do and try to create a work where what matters isn't content, but style. Be bold!

But those things don't really matter that much to me, when all is said and done. My aim is not to prove what a literary pro I am. It's to tell you this story. Granted, I'm very tempted to use one of those complicated styles, interrupting the flow of things. However, I promise that from now on, I'm going to tell you what I want to tell you right off the bat, and I promise not to bore you.

There's a certain other party I should mention in order to round out the details of daily life on the island. The most important neighbors settled here thousands of years before we came, and they are the ones to whom this island truly belongs—the seagulls. Because, you see, it would be impossible to describe the island unless they're included in the story. The same seagulls who savagely shriek as they swoop in and out of the sea, triumphantly bringing ashore the fish they've caught from just below the water's surface. The same seagulls, we've come to realize, who have their own unique language of sounds and frequencies. Those very seagulls who traipse on the stone terraces of our houses some nights, making noises similar to human footsteps.

We had become so intimate with their white shadows that we could almost understand the language they spoke among themselves. We were able to distinguish when they grew angry from the warnings they would exchange among one another, and to discern their cries of lovemaking from those they reserved for scolding their young.

The wisest thing the island's first human inhabitants did was to refrain from frightening or threatening the lives of the seagulls, the primary residents of the island. The seagulls, at that time, probably looked suspiciously upon these strange intruders, subjecting them to a type of test that would last for years—a test that could determine whether they would do harm to their children. A state of harmony was established at last between the humans and the seagulls, between these wild birds and these hermitic people who were seeking refuge from a previous life, agreeing to mutual noninterference by means of a silent pact.

This agreement came to a permanent end one day with the sale of a house. Prior to that sale, none of the houses on the island had ever been sold, because their owners preferred to live in them themselves, or perhaps let their friends use them. But one day, our elderly uncle—that was how we thought of him, though we were unrelated—at Number 24 had a heart attack. The island's much-loved doctor, residing at Number 18, had always cured us of our aches and pains, and never stinted on his endless and noble volunteer spirit. Even so, the doctor was unable to save the old man, whose idler of a son then put the house up for sale.

It was ultimately through the real estate sales ads in the newspapers that we got wind of these events, and not from this good-for-nothing son— who lived in the capital and didn't even show up to bury his father in his grave. But as a result, this event caused one of the biggest waves of excitement on the island, with everyone giving a piece of his mind to this loafer who had put his father's house up for sale merely to have a little more fun in the capital's discotheques, thereby sullying his father's good name. Number 24 had been one of the most admired people on our island. Those of us of the second generation who were in our thirties and forties had shown this man the utmost respect. He had been known throughout his working years as one of the country's most respected and renowned attorneys, having subsequently settled on the island upon invitation by the island's owner, who was also an acquaintance.

Lara and I were among the later arrivals to the island. I ache as I remember her. I'll be telling you about Lara a little later.

During my first days on the island, when I was still figuring out who was who, people would speak with great respect of Number 24, otherwise known as the attorney. They told me that I would be highly impressed by him when I met him. I enthusiastically looked forward to this occasion, but hesitated to disturb him—not wanting to upset the placid life he led. As a result, it wasn't until about a month after arriving on the island that I was able to meet this modest and rather reclusive man—and in the quirkiest of ways, at that.

I had been swimming in the sea with my friend the Writer, whom I'd met during my first days on the island. We were just about to head back to shore when my friend called out to the attorney and told him I was the friend he'd wanted to introduce. The two of us began to swim toward the attorney, who, in turn, had begun to swim toward us. Still swimming toward each other, right there in the sea and in that most ridiculous of circumstances, we proceeded to utter polite words of introduction that would only have made sense if we were fully dressed and ashore: "So pleased to meet you, sir! I've so been looking forward to meeting you, as luck would have it! What an honor!" The attorney, you see, being of the older generation, was speaking in an extremely polite vein and in that deep voice of his, which so stirred our sense of respect. I, in turn, was doing my best not to be outdone.

But then, just as we came face-to-face, a bit of comic mishap occurred. We found ourselves among a swarm of vegetables tossed into the sea from some ship or other—no way of knowing! A cucumber peel attached itself to my mouth. As I was swiping it away with my hand, I was trying both not to swallow any water and to reply to the gentleman in a suitably graceful manner. A smashed tomato had also found its way to the attorney's forehead, where it stuck. And so it was that we experienced this painstakingly polite and formal introduction ceremony, attempting to stay afloat in the sea while we peeled vegetables from our faces and mouths.

Later, in the midst of entertaining conversations on fragrant evenings atop shady terraces, we would look back on this peculiar introduction ceremony of ours and have a good laugh over it. My friend, the Writer, would even say that he was going to write a story based on this amusing encounter, turning phrases both refined and vulgar as he would attempt to wipe off the imaginary eggplant stuck to his eyes.

Despite his somewhat exalted position on the island, he was unable to achieve his dream as a result of the events I'm about to relate to you. The task of summarizing the story has fallen unto me, a mere stand-in who pales in comparison. Though the attorney never mentioned his son, who was around our age, I had the sense that the elder was hurt by his son's neglectfulness and degenerate ways and had found in us a means of fulfilling his fatherly longings.

Three or four days before his death, at the point of day when the sun was directly overhead, he had shared with me that he intended to start jogging. "I've really put on the pounds," he said. "The situation is dire. I'll be damned near unable to budge before long. And yet, just look at those old seagulls! Do they ever give up flying? They just go on flying and swooping through the sky and diving in and out of the sea in their hunt for food. Humankind should follow the example of these intelligent creatures. And for my part, I'm going to jog every day from now on."

I'd tried to warn him, in a facetious way, of the dangers of this sudden twisted inspiration. "You could at least walk, instead of jog," I said. He just laughed. "Well, if I said I'm going to jog, 'walk fast' is what I meant. How could I possibly jog at my age!"

They found the poor man sprawled out on the wooded path at daybreak a few days later. He was unconscious. The doctor who tried to save him said that the attorney had been walking at a pace that had been too much for his heart.

Whenever there was a death on the island, one of two courses of action was taken. Either we would bury the body on the scenic hill we'd set aside as a cemetery, or we would send the body back to the homeland on the ferry that visited the island once a week. But because it was necessary to keep the body on ice until the ferry arrived, as well as on the ride that followed, this wasn't an especially practical method. We sent along the official death notice of the late attorney (as he was now referred to on the island) to the census bureau and ensured its processing through a system set up by his acquaintances a number of years ago. In other words, it's not as though we were doing anything illegal on this forgotten island. We were a settlement unit too small to be appointed a governor from the capital. They had overlooked us.

Oblivion, Abandonment, Loneliness: how truly priceless these notions actually were. How necessary they were to those serene lives of ours. Writing these lines now, I remember those days of yore and I long to sing the lament of the paradise we lost. My heart has been completely torn.

We assumed the matter had come to a close, and that house Number 24 would thus be abandoned to a fate of a sad stranglehold of ivy vines and burgeoning vegetation creeping inside and out. Instead, we were overcome with a rush of excitement when a neighbor who read every detail in the newspapers, even the obituaries, gave us the news: house Number 24 had been put up for sale. Space was made for a glowing account of our island under the heading: "House for sale on island in paradise-on-earth." The sale actually proved to be the end of the small society we'd protected for years, a violation of our privacy, and a disruption of the tranquility we lived in. As a result, there were even some who suggested that we collect money to buy the house ourselves. But having grown soft from our lives of lassitude on the island, we were simply unable to make and enforce the necessary decision. We had lost our interest in such worldly affairs. Our lives contained no traffic jams, bureaucracy, taxes, filling out of forms, banks, and the like. With no more than the pair of shorts we would slip on in the morning—the men typically shirtless like me, the women clad in bikinis and sarongs—we would chat, sip coffee, take the occasional dip in the sea, and go fishing together. At an unhurried pace like slowly flowing water, we were simply going about our lives. The island had numbed us.

One day we saw a boat speeding toward us, splitting the sea in two. It looked like an assault boat. It drew up to the island's pier, and out stepped a group of official-looking men in suits and sunglasses, wireless radios in hand. They stopped for a word with the grocer before taking him along on their way to Number 24. They remained inside for about an hour as one of them took a series of pictures of the house with the large camera in his hand. After having a look around the island, they boarded the assault boat again and took off.

They didn't offer so much as a word or nod of greeting to us. When they were gone, we descended on the grocer, who informed us that the men knew all our names. It was all but evident now that an important person was coming to our island. Someone with state relations, from high up. Or in other words, in the expression we used among ourselves, one of the "large-headed cattle." However, even the most imaginative one among us—that being the Writer—had failed to guess that the one who was coming was the guy at the very top.

Then one day "He" came, and the history and fortune of our island changed forever.

2

MOST OF US had assembled at the pier, consumed with curiosity, as the great white steamer drew toward the island at its usual time Wednesday morning. It was a curiosity that no longer had anything to do with who was coming, because over the intervening weeks, a few workers had come and refurbished the house. They touched up the paint inside and outside the house, tidied up the garden, replaced a broken window or two, and sandpapered and polished the banister and stairs. Actually, their revamping the house to give it a spotless appearance was something we found odd.

The person in charge of this entourage was a well-dressed individual. This man, unable to hide the fact that he was a soldier perhaps due to his impeccably clean-cut attire, kept a strict watch over the workers. All the same, by now we correctly suspected who was coming. Besides which, the workers, being human, had let a few words slip out.

Having fallen from favor after his five-year iron-fisted rule and failed to win reelection, the President had chosen to come here. What an honor! The news had come as a total shock to the lot of us. Why was he coming? What business did he have here? What on earth could someone used to a life of ostentation, ceremonies, and luxury possibly hope to find on this island?

However, the media attention his arrival would attract to the island felt ominous. Worse still, since the President had enemies as well as friends, the island would become a target. He had once come within a hair's breadth of losing his life while traveling in his armored car when a C-4 bomb had exploded on the road, and on two other occasions he had barely escaped the bullets of assassins.

I remember it well: on the eve of the President's arrival, my Writer friend and I had spent the entire night in conversation about our worries concerning this. I'll admit I wasn't as pessimistic as he was. I didn't find it especially out of the ordinary for the statesman to have come to these parts for the sake of a peaceful retirement. Who could say—maybe he was seeking refuge in the desolation of our island, and to rest his tired soul as he lived a simple life, fed up and disgusted with the blur of all the ceremonies, the government crises, the official parades, and the media. Perhaps he'd chosen the island especially for its security. After all, who could come anywhere near such a tiny island and plot an assassination without being seen? My Writer friend considered my assumptions rather naive.

Not being into politics as much as he was, I thought he was blowing things out of proportion. I believed the generally accepted statement that "the President and his friends, who took on the rule of the country to save it from a civil war" had good intentions. Despite our neighbors' fears, which echoed mine, that our island's tranquility would be disrupted, we nevertheless agreed that we should extend the President our respects.

With this on our minds we assembled at the pier and looked on as suitcases and an assortment of furnishings were hauled from the ferry onto the motorboat—the same one that always arrived with our weekly supplies. The three people to step out of it grabbed the suitcases and boxes and began to make their way to Number 24.

The motorboat returned to the ferry, and, from what we could make out, a few people wearing white climbed aboard, painstakingly assisted by official aides. The President, undoubtedly, was the one wearing the straw hat. As the motorboat approached, we saw that we weren't mistaken. The President was clad in a white suit, gleaming and immaculate, with a gray tie around his neck. The strong-willed face we'd seen hundreds of times and had come to know so well from his pictures in the newspapers was heading our way. At last the motorboat was tied to the pier. Assisted in the same manner as before by the officials who respectfully offered their hands, the President set foot on our island. He clasped a stylish cane in his hand. Following behind him were an elderly woman dressed in white who we guessed was his wife, along with two children, a girl and a boy, who appeared to be around the age of twelve or thirteen.

We casual islanders on the pier were no fashion match for such a smartly attired family. Hell, we were downright dumpy—some of us dressed in no more than a bathing suit, some in a pair of shorts, while even the most pulled-together among us sufficed with shorts and an undershirt. Among the women, too, the dress code consisted of a bathing suit or something with shorts, with colorful skirt-wraps used by a few of the bikini-clad to cover themselves below the waist.

The conditions and the climate that people live in tend to change people. After all those years on the island, ties and jackets and the like had become nuisances that bound and gagged us. Over time, we had begun to dress like the natives of some tropical island and had become oblivious to that reality. Even as we imagined how peculiar we must have looked to the President, we couldn't help but be filled with horror at the sight of his clothes— particularly the tie so tightly wound beneath the flaccid waddle of his chin.

Setting foot securely on the pier, the President leaned on his cane and, giving us the once-over like a conquistador just setting foot on the American continent and encountering the half-naked natives, he yelled in a booming voice, "Greetings, my friends!" It was a tone of voice that was all too familiar to us, echoing back from days of yore, and in particular from our days of military service. Not unlike a military squadron facing an inspection and unaware of how ridiculous we would appear, we were involuntarily and unthinkingly prompted to retort: "Thank you, sir!" Our Writer was nowhere to be seen, but as we knew him to be secretive and curious, he was probably spying on us from some secluded hideaway in the forest. In retrospect, it's not that I wasn't made uncomfortable by this retort of ours that I mention; the events unfolding on the pier were so out of the ordinary that we actually found them fun.

The President had begun to shake our hands one by one, so we got in line. His wife followed, shaking our hands too. As for the children, they were looking forward to the end of this terribly boring business. By the way, there's something I forgot to mention (and there may be other things as well): when I was giving you an introduction to the island I didn't mention that there were no children. Living here was unsuited to families with school-age children, although some families' children or grandchildren would come to visit during their summer vacations, returning home in time for school. So these children must have been the President's grandchildren, here for their summer vacation.

Oh, you precious island of ours! Forgive us for having done you such harm, for shaking our enemy's hand in deference, and even with a slight bow—after all the munificence you've shown us!

And you, too, my Writer friend. Forgive us for not having listened to your warnings from the very first day and for blaming you for what we thought was needless pessimism!

I have no way of knowing where you are now—whether you're free, whether you're suffering in some cell somewhere, or whether you're dead or alive, but in the event what I'm writing should ever find its way to you, I want you to know how shameful I feel, and how much I miss you.

If only it were possible to go back to the beginning, to erase these events. If only the President had never come to the island—or if only we had never greeted him at the pier, bending over backward to express our respects to him and his wife as we accompanied them to Number 24. But we did, and as if this weren't enough, that evening at our humble garden café we held a welcome party that flowed with freshly caught fish and our locally made white wine. Though I blush with discomfort at the thought of these things, there's no way to get around the fact that Number 1, an innocuous and mild-mannered man we had pressured into making a welcome speech, even raised a toast in honor of our new neighbors. I'm still aghast at the way we all shot up out of our seats, shouting, "Welcome!"

Responding to our hospitality, the President stood up to make a speech.

"My dear neighbors," he pronounced with very august demeanor. "My wife and I would like to express our sense of indebtedness and gratitude for this extraordinary acceptance ceremony on our first day on the island. I've experienced enough summers, winters, autumns, and springs to know that each and every corner of our nation is a paradise. Yet your island really is in a league of its own and possesses an intoxicating beauty. It is my belief that following my long years in the fray, there couldn't be a more suitable place for my wife and myself to spend the simple and modest life we wish to live, and that we've found the right place. And so it is in the name of God's mercy that I commemorate my late friend and the original proprietor of this island. He had mentioned it to me years ago, even inviting me to build a house of my own, at the same time the first one was being built here."

At this point in his speech, we all looked at Number 1 in an effort to discern whether he had any knowledge of his father's invitation, but he was listening with at least as much amazement as we were.

"Caught up in the struggles of that era," continued the President, "not only was I unable to accept his invitation, but I wasn't even able to find the time to see the island. I must admit, however, that the things he told me about the island stayed with me, turning into a secret regret that would haunt me from time to time. That's why, in running across the newspaper ad announcing that a house had been put up for sale on the island just as I was about to retire..." (We noticed here that he said "as I was about to retire," rather than "as I was about to be made to retire.") "...I was convinced that this was nothing less than a sign from God."

And so the speech continued, at the end of which the President, taking his wife by the hand and having her stand up alongside him as he raised his glass in a toast, regaled us with flattering words along the lines of "We're one of you now. What's ours is yours and what's yours is ours. We are so proud that you've accepted us as your neighbors!"

WHAT NAIVE, stupid, and clueless creatures we were. The President's speech, as exciting for us as for those who had heard his many hundreds of speeches in the past, filled our heads with beneficence and friendship, and led us to embrace them as a sweet elderly couple who presented us an honest and good-hearted manner. Over coffee following dinner, the ladies of the island had gathered round the President's wife, who addressed the group of women with the same presiding air as her husband. Then again, maybe it wasn't the two of them who were putting on airs, but we who saw them as having those airs. It was quite a lovely evening, so refreshing from the mild air and the tiny droplets of water blowing in from the sea, licking our faces.

If only...if only Poseidon himself had bellowed from the darkness of the sea that night, unleashing malevolent storms upon us, smashing that godforsaken ceremony to smithereens. If only the pantheon of monsters at the depths of the sea had laid siege upon us. (Could this be another one of my overly flowery sentences, I wonder? Too literary? Whatever—the editor will take out the unnecessary paragraphs anyway, in the event these chicken scratches of mine end up published someday.)

I suppose there's no need to point out that the Writer had skipped out on this meeting. He was the only one on the island who had yet to meet the President. I had the impression the Writer was swearing a blue streak at us in his anger—a prospect that weighed on me heavily. But what was I to do; it's not as though it was up to me to steer the course of events. How could I have adopted such a decisive attitude so early on? In the end, I did what everyone else was doing. I didn't dwell on it much, really. I simply fell in step with the rest. This isn't exactly something to be proud of, but in hindsight, I don't know what else I could have done.

3

A S THESE EVENTS unfolded, two days went by with no sign of the Writer. No one came to open the door the couple of times I stopped by his house. I couldn't be sure whether he was actually away or he was ignoring me to punish me, but there was no question he was mad at me. He was neither calling me nor anywhere to be seen, distancing himself from our daily visits.

One morning, two days later, I found him in a place we called Purple Water. Of the handful of locations suitable for swimming on our island, each a cove lined with pebbles, one was called Purple Water, one by the name of Lara, and the other, Deep

Water. We would get together to go swimming at whichever one was the least windy and had the fewest waves, which varied by the day. The other coves were set aside for the seagulls. We would keep out of the areas where they lived. On these banks, the seagulls would lay their eggs, brood, protect their young, build nests out of leaves and shrubs, and go about their lives as a wild species that maintains its distance from people.

Given that the wind was blowing from the west that day, I should have chosen to go to one of the other coves besides Purple Water. All the same, I headed there on an odd hunch. It's possible I'd anticipated that the Writer would act on a sense of the contrary, not wishing to see any of us. It turns out I was not mistaken. I found my friend on Purple Water cove, looking out at the reddish-blue waves for which it was named, making an attempt to gather his long hair as it scattered about in the wind.

Though he heard my footsteps, he didn't bother to turn around to see who was approaching, but he probably suspected it was me.

In silence, I sat down beside him. We watched as the swelling sea rushed at us, repeating its timeless tidal game, and the seagulls as they dove in and out of the sea. Then I asked, "You remember the introduction with the attorney here?"

"Sure I do!" he said.

"What a kick we got out of that, huh?"

"We did."

"An honor to meet you, sir!" I said, pretending to pull something out of my mouth and throw it away. But he didn't laugh, after which there was more silence. He absentmindedly drew various shapes of some kind among the pebbles with the twig in his hand.

I could sense his anger beneath the calm appearance. He was so tense that I could almost see the muscles ripple in his wiry body.

The silence went on for a while. Then I said:

"In your opinion, if someone is treated badly, would it be right for that person to treat the other guy the same way?"

He paused before answering, as though weighing whether or not to respond to this question, then said, "It depends on who it is!"

We were quiet again. Then our conversation took an odd turn.

"Are you saying that it's right to respond to those who've done you wrong by treating them the same way?" I began.

"What are you getting at?"

"Wouldn't this be to repeat the very same thing they've done to you?"

"Are you really that gullible? Or are you putting me on?" He turned and looked at me for the first time.

"I may be gullible, and I may not be as familiar with politics as you are, but whatever he may have done..."

"You really have no idea what you're talking about."

"...he's human too!"

"Get real! You've lost your senses!"

"Maybe so, but what are you going to do in a case like this? Should we just throw the two old farts in the sea? And their grandkids, too?"

"As if that'd be enough!" I heard him mutter through clenched teeth, the intensity of the hatred within him making me shudder. I could see that an obstacle too great to be bridged by talk had wedged its way between us, and yet, I couldn't get over my wish to be able to agree with him and for the two of us to grow closer. It was because I cared for him with all my soul. I could hardly have told him this, given that he wasn't fond of overly familiar expressions. But at least I can admit this here: he was the friend I valued most in life. Often, in the sea on Deep Water Beach, we would stand at a distance from each other and dive underwater, finding each other in the depths and grabbing each other's hands before bursting triumphantly to the surface, just like a couple of kids. Four clasped hands would emerge at first, followed by the rest of our bodies. Knocking back a couple of glasses of wine late in the afternoons, either in his garden or mine, we'd talk about literature, life, and people. Yet he would never talk about his past. Who was he? Why was he living alone? What had he done before coming to the island? To him, these were taboo topics, and his life was a subject he simply wouldn't discuss. Whenever the conversation came around to it, he would get testy and change the subject.

My girlfriend, with whom I'd been living on the island for many years, was every bit as crazy about him and wished to do something about his loneliness. Yet it was a wish the circumstances on the island could not accommodate; besides, the Writer appeared to have no complaints with the situation. It was as if there were a layer within his personality consisting of a medieval suit of armor, and there was just no getting past it. He tended to be a man of few words, his finely featured face bearing a troubled expression even when he laughed. It was only when he talked about literature that I would ever see it light up.

I should also add that he was always a ruthless critic. I would bring him some of the essays I'd written and ask him for his opinion. He'd answer with something like: "Is your name Marcel?" "No!" I'd reply. "But you write like Marcel Proust," he would continue. "You've tried to produce a Proustian text, but don't forget, there's a world of difference between being Proust and being Proustian. This here is a style based on a Parisian writer by the name of Marcel who found himself within a set of conditions unique to his own life; it was his own style and his own voice. You would do well to find a narrative voice of your own. Otherwise, even if what you write is better than Proust, it'll remain no more than an imitation of Proust."

For some reason, I would never take offense at being criticized by him like this, pressing on instead with renewed enthusiasm as I shut myself up in my study and wrote something else. Invariably he would blurt out: "Shame on you!" wagging his finger with a menacing scowl. "I caught you this time, too. Is your name Jorge Louis? Have you been reading Borges recently?"

I would blushingly admit that yes, I had been reading Borges, that I had been immensely impressed by him, and wished to write something in the same vein. "Don't forget your own voice!" he would say again. "That's what matters most. Your voice is yours! It's a style that's completely yours. It flies in the face of any other style or fashion in the world, no less a part of you than your hands, your eyes, the expression on your face, or your laugh."

My dear friend, my merciless teacher: What would you make of these lines if you were able to read them now, I wonder? It may be that this is the first time I'm writing the way you'd wanted me to write, steering clear of the templates of stylistic essays and without attempting to imitate anyone else, but simply telling the story as myself—no matter how clumsy it may be or how awkward it may look, even if I make no sense at times, and even if none of it should have any literary value. The difference being that this time, I'm overcome with the woes of the tale I need to tell. Remember how you used to say that every story finds its own style? Well, I think that's what's happening here. As I tell it, the story—the novel—is actually finding its own style and voice.

You must have taken a bit of pity on me at the end of that tense conversation on Purple Water, because you said this to me with great consternation:

"Look, I know you aren't into politics, but you just don't have the right to close your eyes to the world you live in as much as you have. You know that for years the country has been bleeding and polarizing, and that people are being split up into opposing camps and pitted against each other, right?"

"Of course I do!"

"And you know that with the seeds of hatred sown among them, ethnic and religious groups have gone on killing each other without end, only inflaming the blood feud all the more!"

"Of course!"

At this point in the conversation, you stood up and said to me, raising your voice:

"You know everything, my friend, and yet, you still don't know who tore our people asunder, who started this blood feud, who wanted it and planned for it to happen."

You took off then, leaving me alone at Purple Water. And all I could do was stand there, staring after you.

Clearly, that was a day we wouldn't be returning to Deep Water, seeking each other's hands in the depths of the sea.

4

I can't say I remember anything in particular about the first days the President and his family settled on the island. They had retreated into their house, and we rarely saw them. By all appearances, life on the island had once again turned subdued, flowing at a trickle as it always had. There was only one difference. That difference, specifically, was that there were three additional people staying on the island, ostensibly to help the President's family settle into their new home. They slept in an official boat drawn up to the shore. We surmised, as we had in the past, that they were military personnel, dressed in civilian clothing.

Wearing dark sunglasses and bearing a disciplined and serious air, these young men kept their distance from the islanders, never speaking with us nor establishing any relations with us. They even dined on the boat instead of obtaining their provisions from the grocer. It didn't escape our attention that they were making thorough rounds of the island, taking notes as they went about a meticulous process of inspection, perhaps assessing the possible dangers before the President and the level of security on the island. The truth is, we weren't paying all that much attention to them, knowing that their stay on the island would be a temporary one. We were in good spirits again, convinced by now that the new neighbors wouldn't be able to change life as it was on the island. And with the island being so remote from the mainland, there was no risk of being surrounded by reporters. Maybe the President had made the right choice for himself.

I had had the opportunity to think long and hard about what the Writer had said following our conversation at Purple Water. About this he was right: our beloved country, famous for its purple mountains, its steep cliffs, its blue seas, and its peaceful people, had for years been hit hard by endless internal conflicts, with no one able to put a stop to the violence. Upon reading the newspapers that were delivered each week, we would feel devastated with sorrow, unable to make any sense of how this passion for violence had spread throughout the country. Ethnic groups, religious sects, armed organizations, and regional powers were fighting both the state and each other, within the beautiful country we remembered from our childhood as untroubled and serene.

Sometimes one of these groups would side with the state, attacking its opponent, only for the state to form an alliance with one of the other groups in the event that something changed. There were frequent reports of torture-related deaths taking place in prisons, in which hundreds of thousands were under arrest. The foreign press was constantly reporting the human rights violations being committed in our country, as well as censuring the ruling government. How these people who had once lived together in harmony could turn into bloody enemies was beyond our comprehension. It was apparent to us that these groups would never be able to return to their former state of friendship; nor would they ever be able to live together again.

These reports would leave a bitter taste in our mouths, and yet, with a selfishness we hardly admitted to ourselves, much less to each other, we would think: "Good thing we came here and got away from all that!" We were God's fortunate mortals, indeed.

Whenever we would read about the President in the newspapers, it was invariably as "the Nation's Father" and savior. In the official speeches he would give every now and again, he would say that it was foreign powers and enemy nations' fifth-column activities that had fomented this rift and pushed us to the edge of disaster. The consolidation of power, he would say, was being carried out for the sake of reestablishing national unity and cooperation. On national holidays we would see him either waving at the people from his convertible automobile or patting a child on the head. At times, the visits he would pay to such places as orphanages and elderly care centers would appear in the press, embellished, without exception, by pictures he would see to it were taken of him as he presented gifts to children or the elderly.

Speaking of pictures: There's one detail from those days that does stick out in my mind, as a matter of fact: the group photo.

But here I've revealed yet another quirk of writing off the cuff and of jumping around haphazardly from one thought to the next, letting the novel unfold through a series of associations. And yet, as will be revealed along the way, the photograph would end up playing a critical role in the course of events.

We were all notified that it was the President's wish to "eternalize" his move to the island by having a group photograph taken with his neighbors, for which we would be meeting at the pier the following morning. Informed of this by the grocer, who had visited each house to pass on the news, I swallowed my pride and went to the Writer.

"Look, sooner or later you're going to have to meet the President anyway," I said to him. "Besides, it's not like you can go on hiding for years. Why don't you just come to the pier with the excuse of having our pictures taken, meet him briefly, and that'll be the last you'll ever have to see of him." I must have managed to convince him that if he didn't show up, he'd only be drawing even more attention to himself, and that the President wouldn't leave him alone, because the next morning the Writer showed up at the pier along with everyone else. No one even noticed him in the crowd. I was the only one to have noticed his absence at the meetings that had taken place up until now, and the President had not yet found the time to meet his neighbors individually.

We took our places, standing as a group. The President's aides had us positioned so that the soft morning sunlight lit up our faces. They moved us into our poses as if they were expert wedding photographers, ensuring that we would all appear perfectly within the frame. Then they set about taking photographs of us from one angle after another with the large, state-of-the-art cameras in their hands.

Oh, this gullible heart of mine! My bloody naivete! The matter of the photograph had seemed to me to be a nice gesture on the part of the President, a symbol of friendship. I was oblivious to the unnatural way the whole business had been carried out, the way the aides had gone to such great lengths to make sure that each and every one of us would be clearly visible in the photographs they took with their professional cameras. I had believed the old man had wished to have his photograph taken with his new neighbors for the sake of creating a memento marking the beginning of his new life.

As if that hadn't been bad enough, I had even believed that by having my Writer friend join the group, I'd managed to prevent a slew of misunderstandings that could have arisen in the future, and actually felt proud of myself for it!

Will you be able to forgive me, I wonder? If only I hadn't insisted, as I did that day, you wouldn't have taken part in this group photograph, nor would all those abominable things have happened to you.

Maybe we would have experienced that hell regardless—maybe we wouldn't have been able to prevent it anyway. But I should have been able to see that the photograph was a trap. Thanks to a vapid act of friendship, I ended up doing you more harm than your shrewd enemy. Now it's too late; there's no way for me to tell you how sorry I am or how much my heart aches with unhappiness; nor would it do either of us any good.

I ought to describe the first minor shock we experienced on the island two days after the photographs were taken. Do you remember the wooded path I mentioned earlier? Our dirt path, lined on either side by majestic trees that stretched up and wove into a canopy overhead, giving it the appearance of a tunnel of green. Soaked with sweat beneath the noontime sun on our way back from the grocer or the pier, we would no sooner set foot on this path than we would find relief in the cool shade of the lush, secluded forests. The canopy above our heads was so dense with foliage that we couldn't even see the sun. This miracle of nature was one of the greatest treasures we had on the island.

What misfortune it was to discover the trees on this path being trimmed one day. With great skill, the President's men were pruning the trees, cutting and shaping each one so as to form two single green walls. Clearly the men possessed physical talent, climbing the trees and cutting the branches that came together overhead with remarkable deftness and speed. By the time we'd heard about what was going on, half of the trees had already been pruned. Assembled on the path, we helpless islanders could only stand there staring in bewilderment as uniform walls were emerging on either side of us. Those trees that had at one time been left to their own natural state had turned into green sculptures of the kind hewn by the gardeners at Versailles. Most horrific of all was that the canopy that had been above our heads was gone, and the path was now exposed to the direct light of the sun. As you might imagine, the first thing we did as soon as we got over our initial shock was to try to stop the men from going any further. But it did no good. "President's order! Talk with him!" they would say, still shearing the trees. They hadn't even bothered to look back at us.

Realizing that our pleas were falling on deaf ears, we ran headlong to the President's house and knocked on his door. "Stop these men now! They're destroying our trees right in front of our eyes!" we were going to say. His granddaughter opened the door. We told her we wanted to see the President at once, and a few of the especially impatient among us may have even ventured their way inside. But the girl looked at us in shock, as if to say, "And just who are you to come stampeding up here to see my grandfather, the President?" But then she spoke with firm assurance: "My grandfather is working. He hates to be disturbed!"

We did all we could to persuade the precocious girl, telling her it was an extremely urgent situation, but it was hopeless: "It is absolutely against the rules for us to go and knock on my grandfather's door while he's working!" she said. "Even I can't go in to see him. Come back at twelve o'clock."

And then she slammed the door in our face. We looked at each other, then ran back to the dirt path. Even if we had been able to meet with the President, it was too late now. Most of the trees had already been pruned, leaving behind the two surgically precise green walls. I wanted to cry. "There must be some mistake here!" Number 1 said. "The President never would have given an order like that! The men must have misunderstood. Otherwise, I just can't imagine why the President would just suddenly destroy all that beautiful foliage—it's the very pride of the island!"

A few others agreed with him. It was probably some terrible misunderstanding; maybe the men had misconstrued the President to have meant the trees on the dirt path, when in fact he'd meant the trees in his own yard. In the end, this was the view adopted by the majority. "Yes, yes!" they said. "This is just a huge mistake! Our President couldn't possibly have given an order like this. It's a shame, but what can we do? Undoubtedly, the trees will grow back!"

I had serious doubts about this explanation, however, unable to forget the things the Writer had said, and unable to forget that he'd accused me of being gullible. But when we arrived to see the President at twelve o'clock on the dot, my suspicions were confirmed.

"See here, my dear neighbors," he explained. "It's possible that after living here all these years, you've grown used to certain irregularities—to some of the turmoil and disorderliness in your midst, as it happened without your really seeing it as such. You've let everything run wild. But human societies can't live this way. Civilization requires people to bring order to their lives and where they live. That god-awful view of the dirt path was the first thing I noticed when I got here. The trees had grown entirely out of control! The way they were all tangled up in each other like that made for a view of this place as anything but civilized. You ought to be grateful to my men for taking care of the matter before they leave. Each time you pass along that road from now on, you'll see those tamed and orderly trees at your sides—pruned, cleared out, and fixed up in keeping with park and garden traditions—and remember what it is to take pride in your island."

We were standing in Number 24's garden, while the President was on the veranda, standing slightly above us. He was wearing white slacks, a gleaming white shirt, and sunglasses, with a pair of moccasins on his feet. He was speaking in that impressive voice of his, his hand in his pocket and his head tilted up a notch. He almost had us apologizing for having left the trees in their natural state, when we'd come there to complain. Number 1 was wearing slacks too, I noticed, when normally he would go about wearing shorts all day. For him to wear slacks was highly unusual.

One or two among us made to object in weak voices, mumbling, "But the green canopy..." or something to that effect. The President cocked his head. "What was that?" he said, bringing his hand to his ear. "I didn't hear what you said, would you say that again?"

At which point, those who had voiced objections had to sheepishly repeat them, louder this time. "Sir, the branches of those trees that used to come together up above us were a wonderful source of shade. But now they're gone. We're as naked under the sun as a monkey's bottom!" they said.

"Hmmm," said the President, scanning us pensively. "So there's a difference of opinion among us. Our views diverge on some issues," he said. "This is natural, and it's good I've found out about it. People can work out their differences by talking about them. Then allow me to give some thought to this matter, my dear neighbors. I believe I'll have a proposal for you shortly."

At that point, we immediately began to speculate as to what this proposal would be as we each made our way back home. It was the President who set the island's agenda now.

As for the Writer, who had been keeping away from us in recent days, roaming around among the cliffs and crags like a wild seagull and sitting on the shore throwing rocks in the sea, he had only one thing to say when I went to his house that evening and told him what we'd just been through:

"You ain't seen nothing yet, my naive friend!"

5

I T WAS SIMPLY IMPOSSIBLE for us to get used to the dirt path in its newly naked state. Whenever we crossed it, which was at least three times a day, we felt no different from people whose heads had just been shaved and who were in shock with the sensation of baldness. The sun shone on our naked heads in all its fury. The seagulls must have been at least as confused as we were, because flocks of them kept swooping over the path, over and over again, as if to check whether the interlaced tree branches that had once blocked their view of the ground were actually gone. They also darted at lightning speed over me a couple of times.

These birds are swift, and when they come near you, they are genuinely frightening. When you see them from far away, their white bodies and the way they gracefully glide through the air—even their shrieks—may remind you of the sea, but in actuality you would be afraid if you were to see them up close. This is because they're savage-looking animals of prey that rarely come near humans. If our experience with them on the island is any indication, they're also very intelligent. Both their instincts and their talent for learning are highly developed.

I remember once reading about an experiment on the subject of switching the eggs of two different species of seagulls. The nine hundred baby birds to hatch from the eggs of the silver seagulls, which migrated annually, and from those of the black-backed seagulls, which never migrated, were raised by the mothers of the other species. Then they tracked the migration patterns of these fledglings.

They found that the fledglings that belonged to the non-migratory mothers and fathers, following their false parents, migrated to France and Spain. As for the migratory seagulls raised by the non-migratory mother and father, they migrated anyway, out of instinct. This experiment proved that both the instincts and the learning talent of seagulls are highly developed. Since our seagulls were of the non-migratory species and weren't raised by the wrong mothers and fathers, the island was their permanent home.

While we would read about these fascinating facts and talk about the seagulls, there wasn't a single one among us who could go near them. We had been sharing the island, and each species lived in its own corner without disturbing the other. The most significant relationship we had with the seagulls was, if you could call it this, our "bribe," which we'd offer them whenever we went fishing. We'd evolved the habit of throwing a mackerel or two and sometimes coral fish or pickerel at the seagulls that would surround our bounty-filled skiffs on the way back to shore. They had grown so used to this business that if we ever failed to throw them any fish, they would swoop down on us, almost as a threat. This situation had led to a curious game between us. And then there were the many memorable times we would hear them walking on our terraces.

But following the sudden pruning of the trees, the seagulls were slicing through the air with such ferocity that it made us nervous. Of course, since we were used to it, we didn't really mind this kind of behavior, because ultimately they had never done anyone any harm. But, unfortunately, it could stir panic in anyone who wasn't used to the seagulls. After the trees were cut back, the matter took a serious turn for the President's granddaughter. The poor girl ended up paying for her grandfather's sin.

Apparently the seagulls swooped down on her as she was eating a candy bar on her way home from the grocer. She instantly panicked and began to run home, trying to protect her head with her hands. In the midst of this commotion, her foot got stuck on a shorn tree branch, causing her to tumble to the ground and badly injure her left arm. When they found her, she was screaming at the top of her lungs and thought the seagulls were still coming down on her. As if this serious scare weren't enough, her arm, twisted and badly sprained, turned as purple as an eggplant the next day. Though our doctor friend carefully bandaged it and placed it in a sling, the healing process was not a quick one.

We were all deeply saddened by this misfortune and even thought to visit the President to express condolences on behalf of the island community, but in the end, we didn't have the guts to do it. We were unable to find a chance to convey our sorrow concerning the misfortune that had befallen his granddaughter, and to pass on our best wishes for the girl's recovery, until two days later, when he called us to a meeting.

The flyer distributed to each of our houses by the grocer (a practice unprecedented in the island's history) requested our presence at the garden café at six o'clock the next evening. It was signed at the bottom by the President.

Receiving this written invitation aroused an eerie nostalgia in me that I wasn't accustomed to. I used to receive numerous summonses, invitations, tax notices, and the like during the years I lived in the capital, but it was all so long ago. There were some among us who would take a ferry back home every so often and stay for a few months, but I hadn't gone in ages. I didn't miss the noisy streets full of automobiles, the bars, the movie theaters, the crowded restaurants. Or perhaps I only thought I didn't miss them. The summons to the meeting that the grocer had delivered brought back all the pomp and circumstance of the city's commotion. I slept fitfully that night.

The next day we met at the café at six, the Writer included. There was the President, sitting right in front of us, attired in white as before, his capillaries visible through his clean-shaven, youth-fully pink-white skin. The café's tables were placed together and lined up so as to form a square. The President was sitting in the very center of one of the outer edges. I noticed that there had been an increase in the number of people wearing pants. A few more of our neighbors had joined ranks with Number 1.

As we entered the bower, we offered the President and his wife our condolences, expressing how sorry we were indeed for them to have met with such a bad stroke of luck so soon after their arrival on the island. We also expressed our wish to apologize even though it hadn't been our fault, along with our wish for a swift recovery for the adorable girl... Well, that wasn't, in fact, what we thought of that insolent know-it-all of a girl, finding her rather tedious, but this was how one had to speak. Our wishes were received with disdain but with an understanding attitude.

Once we had all taken our seats, the President, in his typically fluid manner of speech, apprised us of matters of import. First he explained his thoughts on general subjects such as what civilization is, how human societies should live, and law and order; then he said, "In discussing the pruning of the trees the other day, some of your friends made it clear that they disapproved of this measure." Scanning our faces with his eyes, he then asked, "Is this true?"

"It is!" we said.

"Good," he said. "So that means there are differing opinions on this island about how to live and how to run the island. Is this true, friends?"

He was searching our faces again.

"It is!" we said in unison.

"Thank you!" he said. We couldn't understand why he'd said thank you.

"Friends, what do you call a system in which everyone expresses a different opinion and it is impossible to reconcile these differing ideas with the social order?"

We were unable to give a response to this question as readily as we had to the others. One or two of us blurted out "the opposition," and other blather along these lines. Someone said, "a multiparty regime." Yet another, who was *really* clueless, even let slip with something like "terror." Pressured by a sense of being interrogated, we all had to say something, what with the President's eyes boring into us, and given that to fail to provide an answer would have been something akin to winding up guilty.

"No, my dear neighbors," he said. "I'll tell you what it is; it's anarchy! Anarchy! A system in which everyone expresses a different opinion is called anarchy. Is this true?"

"It is!" we shouted this time, in unison: But if I've said "in unison," I mean it somewhat loosely, because the Writer, sitting at the end farthest from the President and whom I would notice out of the corner of my eye every so often, kept his gaze riveted to a point on the table in front of him, as though lost in scrutiny of an insect he'd found there.

Upon a few people's requests, the grocer approached the tables at this point with a tray carrying tea and water. "No!" the President said in a strident voice, stopping him. "Do that later! We're in the middle of a serious meeting right now. A person won't die if he goes without tea or coffee for half an hour—will he, friends? Is this true?"

"It is!" we said again.

"Look," he said, "let's get straight to the point. As with any other human society, the residents of this island would also not want to live in anarchy, right?"

"They wouldn't!"

"Good! This situation has led me to think. Given that there are differences of opinion on fundamental issues on our island, I've come to believe that the way to get rid of these differences is to bring government to the island. According to what I've learned from my neighbor"—he was nodding toward Number 1—"there's never been an executive committee on this island. Everything's always gone unsupervised. Is this true?"

"It is!"

All these rounds of "it is" were starting to get tedious, making our heads swim.

"This island needs an executive committee, my friends," the President continued. "An administrative committee that, when necessary, will render decisions about the island, ensure that life proceeds in a state of greater peace and without anyone being disturbed, and nip differences of opinion in the bud. Moreover, there are procedures for creating such a committee. These procedures will, of course, be democratic. Democracy is the presiding principle. Is that so, friends?"

"It is!"

At this point my eyes fell on where the Writer had been sitting. He had quietly slipped out without anyone noticing him. What an interesting man, I thought; instead of opposing the President's words, he just walked off. For this, I even disapproved of him a little.

"This group gathered here today amounts to a general assembly," continued the President. "It is incumbent upon the general assembly to form from among its members an executive committee in which it will vest authority. I think this committee should be composed of five people."

"It should."

"Are there any volunteers? If so, have your names written down, and we'll take a vote."

The President's men, who had been milling about in our midst throughout the meeting, prepared to take down names, pen and paper in hand, but no one said a word.

The President asked us once more if anyone among us wished to volunteer. Again, silence. Then, Number 1 raised his hand and asked to speak.

"The floor is all yours!" said the President. "Is there something you wish to say?"

"Yes, my President, I think that you should be the President of this committee."

One or two people applauded in a show of approval, but with a raise of his hand, the President said, "Stop!" and silenced them. "The executive committee hasn't been created yet. Everything needs to be done according to procedure." Then, on seeing that no one had anything to say, he said,

"However, based on all my years of experience in government administration and my many years in service to the state, I'm honored to inform you that I'm prepared to devote this love of service and the benefit of my experience to the service of my neighbors on the island. A duty is a duty; there are none too small, nor too great. It's all in the name of our island!"

He said these last words with such force that we all broke out into applause. The President asked one last time whether there were any volunteers for office among us. We were again silent. Since we had been removed for so many years from these kinds of bureaucratic nuisances, it wasn't easy for us to adapt to the new situation. The President, noting our silence, said, "I have a proposal. I'd like to nominate Number 1, in his capacity as the owner of the island, as a permanent natural member of the committee."

"Well, well, well!" cheered the general assembly. "All right, Number 1!"

We approved the nomination with applause. Then, straightening up from his seat, Number 1 said, "Friends, I thank you for the confidence you've shown in me. I promise to do all I can to be worthy of the paradise that our island is. It's all in the name of our island!" We saw his eyes well up with tears and heard his voice tremble, which filled us with emotion in turn. We had grown so excited, as a matter of fact, that we were all on the verge of crying out something like "May our lives be sacrificed in the name of the island!"

The President turned to Number 1 and said, "Congratulations!" Then he added, "I gather from your courteous applause that two of the committee's five members have now been elected. At this juncture we're going to elect the remaining three people; however, I'm someone who believes that women have a place next to men in a democratic and modern society. Our esteemed women, our mothers, our wives, and our sisters, should take part in public life and take on significant duties. I therefore wholeheartedly urge that we elect a woman to our committee."

Number 1 took the floor again and said, "My esteemed President, thank you for sharing these noble thoughts of yours with us. I would like to nominate your esteemed wife as the third member. After all, she's the most experienced among the ladies on our island and is knowledgeable about these matters."

We applauded.

The President's chubby wife, her eyes half-closed, expressed her thank-you with a calm nod of acknowledgment and did not make a speech.

"Congratulations, ma'am!" the President said. Then he added: "Since there are no other volunteers, we'll determine the remaining two people by drawing lots." He made a gesture with his hand and one of his well-trained men came running, a black plastic bag in tow.

At this point a devilish thought passed through my mind, as I recalled the Writer's doubting words. It occurred to me that three out of five of the committee's members had already been elected at this point. I had my suspicions that Number 1 was in cahoots with the President. Yet we were watching these events unfold no differently than we would an amusing play at the theater, not taking them all that seriously. What harm could possibly come from the executive committee of a tiny little island like ours? The President was, perhaps, manufacturing a game to keep him busy in the face of the void left by the loss of his post with the state administration. Yes, it was all theater, nothing more. This explains why we were making a bit too much of a show of our cheers and ovations, joining in on the vaudeville act half tongue-in-cheek, shouting out things like "Bravo!" just to egg everyone on.

The President announced, "What we've got within this plastic bag here is every number from one through forty! When the number is chosen, a person from the corresponding household—not counting 1 and 24—is to take on official duty on the executive committee."

Next we saw the man dip his hand into the plastic bag and pull out a slip of paper. He gave it to the President, who opened it and read it: "Number 37!"

We broke into applause.

The man then gave the President another slip of paper.

"Number 7!"

The President looked around the room, trying to make out who Number 7 was. Everyone looked at each other in silence. I was stunned. I choked on my shock, unable to speak.

"Who is it we have here, then?" the President said. "Would our friend, Number 7, please stand up."

No one said anything, and I raised my hand. "Yes?" the President said.

"Sir," I said, "our friend, Number 7, was feeling somewhat unwell and had to leave the meeting. If you'll allow me, I'll inform him of the situation."

There was another round of applause from everyone.

My dear friend, the Writer, had thus been made a member of the President's executive committee.

I felt a knot form in my stomach just then, I must admit. After the meeting ended, I spent a long time turning matters over in my head, staring out at the sun as it became a ball of flames being buried at sea. It was a trace, perhaps, of an ominous premonition I felt about your fate. It was the first moment I'd sensed something of what would happen to you down the road. I asked myself, once again, whether people change by virtue of their circumstances, or whether it is people themselves who make their circumstances. Your wish to stay out of trouble, all your precaution, and roaming up and down the hills, your life in public renounced—what difference did any of these make in the end? In spite of it all, here you were, forced to be on the same committee as the President. What luck.

6

AS THE PRESIDENT'S presence in our lives increased a little more with each day, we would remain blind to events, naive as ever in our optimistic interpretations of them. Maybe what they were saying about us was true: we'd turned into a wild bunch of people, living on that island far away from urban civilization. When I look back now, I can plainly see that the source of our complacency was our extreme laziness and lethargy. We weren't ones to protest or take a stand against anything. "May the snake that doesn't bite me live a thousand years!" we would say, unable to take into account that we, too, would come to feel the sting of the snake's bite.

We maintained this attitude of indifference even after what happened to the poor kid who made daily deliveries to our homes. And yet we felt great affection for this young, slow-witted boy who had never seen the inside of a school and who would lose himself in daydreams as he looked off at the horizon when he wasn't working. He had grown up under our care and was like a member of our household. He would distribute necessities like water, bread, and newspapers, which the grocer would keep on hand for us, having them brought to shore with the motorboat. In the mornings, we'd find everything we'd ordered the day before sitting on our doorstep.

This was how it was, up until one day when the boy was seen walking along the main road, crying and covering his eye with his hand. His eye had turned red, as if he'd been punched, becoming black and blue and swelling shut by the next day. There was no way for him to tell us what happened, because he couldn't speak. As always, he retreated into a quiet corner, preferring to keep to himself. We were sharp enough to sense that this business had had something to do with the President or his men, but there were some among us for whom the notion was preposterous, while others of us were too afraid to even think about it.

The incident remained a secret up until the next summons. The summons—which was distributed this time to our houses by the boy's father, the grocer—spelled it out in black and white. It explained that the boy had violated all the principles of security and privacy in the world by being so shameless as to set foot on the President's terrace the other morning, and was therefore being punished for it.

New rules concerning the matter had been put into effect by the executive committee:

1. No one is to approach a house beyond the designated security border and private property threshold of six meters without advance notice.
2. Service personnel in charge of distributing supplies are to fulfill this task between the hours of nine and eleven every morning and in accordance with the property border rules stipulated above.
3. Any and all persons violating these rules established by the executive committee

will be severely penalized by the island's homeowners.

His eyes brimming with pain, the boy's father would later tell us that his son had been on his way to the President's house to deliver the milk and candy bar ordered the day before. No doubt out of a sense of the new hierarchy on the island, he'd begun his rounds with the President's house. Having gotten off to an early start, he was just about to leave the milk at the terrace gate when he was sent sprawling to the ground with a punch in the eye by someone who'd suddenly darted out of the garden. Trying not to wake the residents, the man had asked him in an angry whisper who he was and what business he had there, then let him go.

These events had shown us that even on our peaceful and secluded island, the President lived in tremendous fear, so much so that he kept a guard on duty in his yard—a fact that truly baffled us. The motorboat was still moored to the pier. We had no idea how much longer they were going to stay.

WHEN I ASKED the Writer whether he was aware of this development, given that he was now a member of the executive committee, he waved his hand as though shooing away a fly and said, "Hell no! The devil take him! I haven't been to a single one of those damned meetings yet. And if I do go, God only knows what I'd do."

While no one was admitting it, the tension on the island was growing more palpable by the day, and the road, stretched out beneath the sun like a dried-up riverbed, was filling us with unease.

Late one night, the tension hit a new high. Waking up to the sound of gunshots, we ran helter-skelter out of our houses, still clad in our underwear as we tried to make sense of what was going on. We were consumed with a panic the island had never seen. Even the seagulls, normally calm at night, were shrieking as they flew hither and yon.

Full of fear and concern, we ran toward the President's house when a few people noted that they'd heard three shots fired from that direction. We considered it unlikely, but could the President have been right about his fear of terrorism? Had there been a raid on the island?

A group of men and women made up of the residents who lived closer to the President's house had gathered in his yard by the time I got there. "A terrorist was walking on the terrace," the President was explaining. It was something of a relief to see that he was safe, but it wasn't enough to rid us of the questions in our heads. How could terrorists have come to an island as remote as ours? Where could they possibly hide? The President's men were looking us over like enemies as they clutched their guns, no longer feeling a need to conceal them. Met with these looks, we could only appear sheepish out of some sense of guilt. My horrified neighbors, upset and half-naked, were doing their best to comprehend what had just happened. Even the Writer was there.

"Don't be upset," the President said in the manner of a hero wishing to mollify his people after they had experienced a brush with grave danger. "This is a serious situation, but, thank God, as you can see, the terrorist or terrorists haven't harmed us! They've tried to get rid of me many times in the past, but with the help of great God above, they were unsuccessful at every turn. I've grown used to this state of affairs by now; I see it as the price I have to pay for having served my country. Yet I must admit that these events have a terrible impact on my family, and most of all on my dear grandchildren. I must regretfully inform you at this juncture that the entire island— the bottom of every tree, every nook and cranny, every cave, and, unfortunately, every house—is to be searched, one by one. Our security personnel are going to find these traitors wherever they're hiding and interrogate them. If they put up a fight, they are to be swiftly punished. I apologize to my innocent neighbors for the disturbance we'll be causing them, but if there are any among them who are involved in these events, they're going to pay the heaviest possible price for it."

Panicking, bewildered, and dazed, we went on listening to the speech, still unable to believe what was happening. As if that weren't bad enough, now our houses were going to be searched as well. We were looking at each other in shock, at a loss for what to say or how to react. Their arms wrapped around their grandmother, the President's grandchildren cast their eyes on us with suspicion.

And then, a voice: "Could you tell us a little about how this incident took place, sir? Did someone shoot at you? Did you see anyone? A number of people, perhaps?"

All eyes turned to the Writer. He was talking to the President for the first time, and was possibly the first on the island to ask him a question.

"I'll tell you," said the President. "It was just past midnight. I had just gone to bed. I was about to fall asleep when I heard someone I surmised to be of considerable size stomping about on the terrace. It was obvious that the person who'd come to my terrace at that hour had anything but good intentions." ("So, they got past the guard, too," I thought.) "Then I grabbed my gun as I called out to the terrace and asked who was there," he continued. "But the man just kept walking around on the terrace without answering me. I asked him, 'Who are you?' and 'What are you doing here?' several more times, but he didn't answer. I warned him, saying, 'I'm asking you for the last time, then I'm going to shoot,' but he just ignored me and went on making noise, stomping about. So then I hid behind the column and just held out my arm and fired three shots at random. That's when the noise stopped. I think he ran away at that point, and at any rate, our security personnel who investigated the terrace didn't find anyone there. That's why we have to investigate the island and find this terrorist."

"Sir," the Writer said, "I'm sorry for your misfortune, but would you permit me to ask you one more question so that we may understand the situation?"

The President must have been pleased at the presence of a neighbor who took so much interest in his health, as he then said, "I don't believe I've seen you before, sir!"

"That's right, sir," said the Writer. "I was there when the photographs were taken and for the first part of the meeting at the bowery, but I don't believe I've had the honor of encountering you in person. I've found out that I was elected to the executive committee after I had to leave the meeting to tend to some business affairs."

"Oh, I see!" said the President, "now I remember; so we'll be seeing much more of each other from now on."

It seemed to me that he didn't detect the Writer's bluff, but actually might have been glad instead to have found another tight ally on the island.

"Sir," the Writer said. "If a motorboat were to cross the sea and approach the island, it would be seen immediately, and be heard as well. It's impossible to sneak onto the island. I am therefore suggesting that other possibilities be considered."

"Such as?"

"Such as that it wasn't a terrorist walking on the terrace."

"Who would be walking on the terrace at that hour without evil intent, in your opinion?"

"I don't know but, based on what you've said, the terrorist was quite fond of making noise. He walks around loud enough to wake you up and keeps it up, in spite of your warnings. He doesn't crouch down in a corner, but instead goes on with his stomping—despite your warnings. Does this seem normal to you?"

There was a sense that the President was growing slightly annoyed in the face of the questions being asked by this man he'd assumed was a friend.

"OK, Mr. Detective," he said, "these theories of yours are nice, but they don't change the situation. I repeat my question: What kind of person without bad intentions would walk around on the terrace in the middle of the night and not answer the questions asked of him? Furthermore, why do you think he didn't reveal his identity?"

"Perhaps, Mr. President, he didn't know how to talk."

After recovering from his initial shock on hearing these words, the President then said, "Friends, is there anyone on our island who is unable to speak?"

It had begun to dawn on us by now what the Writer was getting at, given the countless times the seagulls had wandered around on our terraces, but we were developing a habit of answering the President automatically and without commentary. "No, there isn't!" we said.

"You see?" said the President. "Now, let's put an end to fooling around with any more silly questions and let the security personnel begin the necessary inspections."

We thought the talk had ended, but at a moment when we least expected it, the Writer's voice was heard once more:

"I'm terribly sorry, sir, but perhaps the noises on your terrace did not convey a threat."

Frightened out of his wits just a short while ago, now the President had grown irritated in the extreme: "Sir! Sir!" he said. "What is it you're after, here? What dead end are you trying to derail this serious security investigation into? Answer me. What person would walk around on the terrace in the middle of the night—with *no* bad intentions? What kind of person would fail to respond to my warnings that I'm going to shoot?" He stopped, looked at us, and laughed mockingly, his tone full of anger: "Besides, apparently there's no one on the island who can't speak."

"Maybe it wasn't a person walking on your terrace!" said the Writer. "That's why he couldn't answer your questions."

Even in the darkness of the night, I could see a smile spread across the faces of all my neighbors. "What the hell are you saying, man?" the President roared. "What was it then, if it wasn't a person? Could it be there are giant bears living on your island, but I don't know about them? Or then again, maybe it was a dinosaur—could that be it?"

"No sir," the Writer said calmly, "it was a seagull!"

"What seagull?"

"You know, a seagull, sir. Everyone living on this island knows that the seagulls walk around on the terraces at night and that the noises they make in doing so sound much like the stomping of a heavyset man. It really does take people by surprise the first time they hear it. A person may not be able to make sense of how a noise like that could come from this small creature, but maybe because of the way their feet are made, the seagulls make a noise that sounds like the footsteps of a heavy man, and that sound echoes in the night. Right? If you'd be so kind as to allow it, Mr. President, let's do an experiment on the terrace," continued the Writer. "It could even be at the entrance where you're standing now."

Then he began to walk around on the terrace, making stomping sounds, as the President looked on in bewilderment.

"Did the noises sound like this, Mr. President?"

The President must have felt like a commanding officer whose army was falling apart, but even so, so as not to be seen by the islanders as a man who was afraid of seagulls, he muttered with a final effort, "That's ridiculous! Am I a person incapable of distinguishing a seagull from a human being?"

But the voice in which he spoke was much weaker now, his confidence in himself shaken. He could see that we were all in agreement with the Writer and nodding our approval. When even his most trusted ally on the island, Number 1, said, "Yes, sir, the seagulls make this very sound," he swiftly approached the point of giving in, but the Writer had yet to deal his final blow.

Turning to the President's hawk-eyed security aide, he asked, "After the President shot the rounds, did you see a seagull take off into the sky?" "Yes!" the aide replied, at which point we all burst into laughter with the relief of having escaped from a terrorist threat as we stood there in the yard.

There was no longer anything the President could do. Left with no other choice, he accepted the situation, a forced smile emerging on his face. On the heels of playing up his role only moments before as a hero who'd just been the target of an assassination attempt, the President was now in the foolish position of looking like a trigger-happy man who feared seagulls.

"Are we going to search the houses, sir?" an aide obliviously asked. Heading back into his house, the President shouted in a voice full of wrath, "Get the hell out of here!"

From that night forward, he had two great enemies: the seagulls, which were not-so-innocently to blame for his dear granddaughter's sprained arm, and someone who had just finished making a laughingstock out of him in front of his neighbors—that insolent man who'd cleared everything up with his questions—the Writer.

The war was about to begin.

7

I DOUBT THAT ANYONE on the island was able to sleep that night, and indeed, on the heels of all that excitement, we weren't surprised that the lights in the houses stayed on until morning. As for Lara and me, once we got back home, we sat down in the swing for two suspended from the magnolia tree and wrapped our arms around each other. We didn't move, remaining locked in an embrace for a long time. The ominous tension within us and our premonition of bad things to come had taken on a palpable presence, and we were hoping for solace from each other's warmth, too afraid even to breathe. The clean, sweet smell of soap was drifting from her silken brown hair as it blew gently in the soft night breeze.

I had discovered Lara while she was working as a waitress in a cafeteria in the capital years ago. She was so frail, so wounded, and so much like a baby bird thrown out of her nest that my heart began to overflow with tenderness for her. I sensed a graciousness and gentleness about this girl that captivated me as she would shuttle in and out of the kitchen behind the counter, leaving the plates in her hand at the tables with a sad but polite smile, and thanking the customers with a slight bow like a little girl as they paid their bills and left their tips. I had never known until that day that there could be so much tenderness within me. My eyes had begun to give away my emotions with such obviousness that she started turning her head to size me up as she made her rounds of the cafeteria, as if to see if I was still looking at her. I went to that cafeteria again the next day, and the day after, and the day after that.

By that point, we were saying hello to each other and indulging each other with smiles and small talk. It seemed to me that she'd begun to take better care of herself with every passing day, combing her hair more carefully and wearing more eye-catching dresses, and I would feel proud to have had something to do with that. I had just separated from my wife around that time and had little to do. I had been going about my life, a divorced man with no children, stumbling along at my job as best I could, but felt I wasn't liked at the bank where I worked. I was just barely scraping by with the small salary I received, trying to maintain my distance from the country's political conflicts, yet not enjoying life either. Often, I thought of myself as a faceless coward. The most significant action I was able to take within my colorless life was to ask that waitress to join me for dinner on an evening she wasn't working. Her acceptance without the least hesitation was my unexpected reward. My having waited this long, due to my shy nature, may have led her to fear that such a proposal would never come. But she immediately said yes.

On the first evening we met for dinner, she was wearing an orange outfit that suited her to perfection. Her cheeks glowed. I sensed that something was amiss from the tension in the way she'd said, "I can't stay late," but the things I discovered about her as early as that first evening were enough for me to realize that she was suffering deeply in an unhappy marriage. She was consumed with fear, and when I saw her later one day at the cafeteria, I could see from the way she covered her cheek with her hair that she was being beaten by her husband. As our relationship moved along, we began to open up to each other. I found out that her husband was a roughneck involved in shady affairs and constantly in and out of jail, beating her most evenings when he arrived home drunk. The night she told me of these things, tears streaming down her cheeks, we held each other as we sat on the sofa in my bachelor's apartment. A fiery ache welled up from within me as I began to kiss her, and then, as if with a desire to heal each other's wounds, we drifted into making love—deep, tender, and slow, in a way that caressed the bleeding spots in our souls. After that night, rescuing Lara from that man and from that life was all I could think about. I couldn't bear the idea of her being beaten yet again; as time went on, her polite, uncomplaining resignation to her fate only tore me up inside all the more.

We argued about these subjects a great deal. I told her she should divorce him, but she said her husband would never say yes to such a thing, and would undoubtedly break her bones. The only alternative was to run away—but to where? I racked my brains with a thousand and one plans during those days. I even considered robbing the bank I worked for and hiring a murderer to have her husband killed with the money I'd steal. But I knew, even as I hatched these plans in my daydreams, that I would never be able to carry any of them out. The dreams were just a way to console myself and alleviate my sense of helplessness.

Then out of the blue, I remembered the island my elderly uncle had mentioned before he died, and the house he had there. Believing it to be worthless, no one in my family had ever shown any interest in it, figuring there was no use for a house that had been described as something out of a fairy tale. Since it was so remote from civilization that no one would visit it, what use was a dilapidated old house?

It turned out to be the house that made our escape possible. Together, Lara and I erased our traces from that world. We disappeared, and were reborn on this island. Not long after our arrival on the island, with a wish to prove that we would never go back, never return to our old lives, I decided to call my sweetheart Lara, the name of the most beautiful cove on the island. It was a clear, clean cove whose turquoise waters lit up the sand beneath into a special magical world. Just like my sweetheart.

We would never again use her old name. The new name was a good omen, a fresh start.

With its glimmering waters, its cool moonlight, and its scent of jasmine, the island healed us, making us forget our past and delivering us into a new life.

But sitting on the swing in the garden that night, both of us felt a sense of uneasiness we hadn't known since coming to the island.

"So, that evil world isn't so far away from us after all, as it turns out!" whispered Lara. I wanted to calm her with a long, slow kiss. I took her to our bed, which was always a small temple where we could worship our bodies. Now they could cure each other, in an effort to keep the bad memories at bay.

The Writer, however, had neither anyone to cure him, nor anyone to whom he could offer his tenderness. I couldn't find him when I looked for him the next day. Evidently the President had called an urgent meeting of the executive committee early in the morning, and the people elected to the committee were nowhere to be seen. All of us on the island were in suspense and on edge, shooting anxious looks in the direction of the President's house, where the meetings would take place. Nobody knew what sort of new decisions would emerge from this urgent meeting. No one felt at ease anymore. We had nervous discussions in whispered meetings by the sea, in the yards at night, or on late afternoon excursions.

Sweating in agony as they walked beneath the blistering sun because the leafy shade trees on the road had been clipped bare, the majority of the islanders, even if they did not oppose the President directly, were not hiding their apprehension about the way things were going. Some friends of Number 1, who by now had become buddy-buddy with the President, were insisting that it was a good thing that order and discipline had been brought to the island. Outside of these two factions, there were one or two people who weren't hiding their amusement that a little excitement had come to the island. That suggested there was some kind of entertainment value in this state of affairs for everyone.

On that day, I was, I could say, every bit as worried as the seagulls, who also were in a strained state of suspense as they watched over their eggs on the shores set apart for them. Stationed at each egg were two seagulls, which I surmised to be the mother and father. They resembled fortress guards, the way they kept their cautious eyes riveted to the horizon without removing them, even for one second. Since they demanded no friendship or closeness from us, there was nothing we could do other than to leave them alone.

The meeting concluded in the afternoon that day, and in the evening we were all summoned to the garden café for a general assembly meeting. I immediately ran to the Writer. I wasn't surprised to find him in a state of anger. He was swearing a blue streak and kicking the baskets and the legs of the end tables in his apartment. Even after we each opened a beer and sat beneath the grapevines, he continued to curse the President: "The man's gone mad!" he was saying. "He's gone mad for sure. He's insane! If everybody goes along with this maniac, that's it! We're goners! Our living space has been shrinking ever since he got here. Mark my words; eventually we'll be left with no other choice but to leave the island."

After a lengthy attempt to calm him down, I was finally able to bring him around to explaining what had happened. According to what he told me, the President had wasted no time in getting to the point as soon as the meeting got under way. He explained that the seagulls posed the greatest threat to the island. As if it weren't enough that they had taken over the most beautiful banks of the island and were preventing people from using the coves on these sites, these savage birds were attacking people and turning the island into an uninhabitable hell. Thus, the President proposed to the committee that these birds be annihilated. Then he ticked off a long list of ways in which the birds posed a big problem. Since the majority of the committee members apparently sided with the President, they were just about to agree on a measure to wipe out the seagulls when the Writer, unable to resist, took the floor with a strong statement that a subject as critical as this wasn't appropriate for a decision by the committee, but should involve all of the island's residents in a session of the general assembly. Harboring the hope that the island community would be able to consider the issue from a healthier perspective than the committee's knee-jerk response, he insisted on this with considerable determination. Although he knowingly faced the President's obvious hatred, the Writer had put up tremendous resistance against the President's wish to rush this proposal. The Writer said that this was a type of decision that fomented a civil uprising, and that if we were to think of the island as a country, decisions of this nature would fall to parliaments. He didn't mention the matter of the President's granddaughter injuring her arm as a result of needless panic, or of the grown man shooting at seagulls because he was afraid of them. In the end, the Writer was able to get the committee to go along with him, because the President had thus concluded that securing everyone's participation would render a more spirited and effective fight against the seagulls.

After this explanation, the Writer blurted out: "Stand up at the meeting and speak out with me! Surely, no one is going to accept the insanity of this raving lunatic about a war on the seagulls! Try to stop this man from pulling the wool over the islanders' eyes. In fact, start talking to people one at a time, now, before it's too late, and try to stop this madness."

"I will," I replied, albeit rather hesitantly. Talking to the islanders was something I could do, but standing up to talk at the meeting didn't exactly fit my shy nature. I didn't have confidence in myself in this department.

After leaving him, I walked around for a while, then sat on a deserted rock cliff, watching the seagulls for a long time. I looked at the seagulls standing guard over their eggs. Perched in his usual spot at the peak of a sharp cliff, I noticed a familiar old seagull who had made it his habit to stand there, never abandoning it except for when he went hunting. Unaware of any of the arguments currently taking place because of them, these creatures had, for me, an appearance more innocent than humans.

They were grayer when they closed their wings, because their backs were gray. But they were pure white when they were gliding through the air, the underside of their bodies visible then. What sort of fight against the seagulls did this madman have in mind? I realized that I, too, had now begun to think of the President as mad. He had brought us to this point in what had been no more than a week or two.

I ended up sitting on the cliff for nearly an hour. Then I got up and began to make the rounds of my islander friends. Some were in the middle of gardening, while some were napping in their hammocks. Others were returning from the grocer. I told them that the President was about to try to do something insane and that he had decided to wage a fight against the seagulls. I told them we needed to stop it from happening.

"That's crazy!" they said. "What harm are the seagulls! How can you blame them when *he's* the one who's afraid of them?" Evidently, they all felt the same way I did about the matter.

Our friend at Number 12 said, "If he wants to play war games, then let him go find some other island for himself!"

Following these conversations, I went home feeling slightly more at ease, and told Lara about the way things had gone. "The islanders are sensible people; they won't stand for this business!" I said.

She shot me a skeptical look. Her cautious nature, always in anticipation of a catastrophe, had already been shaken by the things the President had done in recent days.

"I hope not!" she said, abbreviating what I'm sure was a much longer response. "But there's one thing I've learned from life: evil is everywhere, and its power is difficult to defeat. Goodness is weak in comparison."

"Don't worry," I said, "we're going to fight with all we've got. Evil will not rule on this island."

Looking into her hazel eyes, I saw no sign that she believed what I'd said. So I felt the need to insist a little more, because I couldn't bear to see her upset. "My love," I said, caressing her brown hair, "maybe you're right—no, there's no 'maybe' about it; you're right—one hundred percent right. In this world, it's evil that is the better organized, and better planned. Besides which, goodness harbors a certain naivete. That's why evil defeats the pure of heart, all over the world. But we've made things just the opposite on this island. I mean, think about it. For all these years, we've had no competition, no fights, and no struggles among us. This is a country for those good people who choose peace. You'll see, our neighbors are going to reject these crazy proposals. And the President is going to get tired of this island, and realize he's unwanted and soon move on."

"What if he forces us to leave?"

"Nothing like that is going to happen," I said. "We're going to defend our way of life, and we're going to stay on this island until the end of time. We won't leave even after we die."

As I waited for my words to soothe her, she suddenly did something that took me by surprise. She kissed me lightly on my lips and then began to cry. The warmth of her lips surprised me as much as her tears, which burst forth like a summer storm.

8

IN THE EVENING, we lined up around the tables that had been placed together in the grocer's garden. To the right of the President sat Number 1; to his left, his wife. The other committee members—including the Writer, I might add, who looked more grim-faced than ever—had taken their seats at the head of the table. I noticed how much Number 1's attire resembled the President's. The man who had wandered around half-naked and barefooted for all these years had now begun to wear pressed white pants and immaculate shirts. Not only that, but he wasn't exactly our only neighbor to be doing this. There were a few others who were wandering around in the same fashion.

I had expected the President to start the meeting, but it was Number 1 who stood up first. "Dear friends," he said. "As you know, we've gathered here today to discuss a very important subject that involves the future of our beautiful island. Our highly esteemed President has come to our island with the experience and ideas that his long years of governing the nation have afforded him. He's brought to light a number of problems that none of us had been aware of, as well as their solutions. I would therefore personally like to present him once again my deep gratitude, and extend to him my applause."

When Number 1 stood up and began to applaud, the other neighbors also stood up and applauded. I stood up as well, to appear to keep in step with everyone else. Only two people were left sitting; my two intimates—my two dearest and true friends—the Writer and my shy sweetheart, Lara.

I wondered whether the President's men noticed this detail as they stood waiting on the sidelines, but their surly expressions and the dark glasses that hid their eyes made it impossible to tell.

After the applause died down, Number 1, having turned his face to the President with a smile, now turned toward us again: "I understand from your courteous applause that you, too, have presented your deep gratitude to our President, and I hereby get the meeting under way. Today, as you've all been made aware, we're going to discuss our island's coves."

We were utterly shocked. Was this supposed to be some kind of game, talking about the coves instead of the seagulls? What were they up to?

"However," said Number 1, "in order to conduct the meeting in accordance with proper procedure, two people each, in favor and against, must first submit their names in writing. It's not as though we can stay in this garden forever, after all now, can we? Speak up, friends, who would like to take the floor on this subject? Don't forget: I'll be giving the floor to two in favor and two against!"

Number 32, whom I had spoken to that morning, stood up and said, "That's all well and good, but how can we know whether we want to argue in favor or against without discussing the matter first!"

Upon which our longtime friend Number 1, who had become more and more like a stranger to us by now, smiled and said, "Those are the rules, friends! It isn't necessary for everyone to speak!"

Then the Writer raised his hand: "I'll take the floor." The President and committee members looked him over with condescending expressions. I felt Lara squeeze my hand, nudging me to get up and speak, and the Writer was looking at me, his eyes fixed upon my face, but what could I have said in front of all these people? I pretended not to understand and said nothing. Instead of me, it was Number 32 who spoke. As for those who spoke in favor, they were two members of the executive committee.

After we were finished, it was the President's turn to speak. He stood up, carefully eyeballed each one of us, and then said only one word: "Civilization!" He continued surveying our faces silently. An ominous stillness lingered in the room. No one was saying a word, and the grocer, after enduring a severe tongue-lashing at the last meeting, was nowhere to be seen. The fact that he wasn't a homeowner barred him from being included in the general assembly.

On the heels of a pause that was just long enough for us to start twitching nervously in our seats, the President, crushing us with his glances, said again: "Civilization!" We didn't have a clue what to do or what direction to look in. Whenever I see people make dramatic gestures in public like that, I feel embarrassed and shrink, seized with a wish to disappear.

At least this time the President didn't make us wait too long:

"Do you know the meaning of this word, friends?"

Once again, he'd put us under his spell and made us feel like students being put to an exam before the strictest of teachers. Who knows how many times he'd used this tactic over the course of his long political career. It was a method at which he was a master. No one said anything, but we all nodded our heads.

"Think carefully. I said 'civilization.' Human civilization. It's what sets people apart from animals, and it's the thoughts, methods, and management styles that give them honor." As if intending to put what he'd said firmly into our heads, he briefly paused once more and continued.

"Constitutions, rules, a free market, entrepreneurial freedom."

Again we nodded as if to agree. And at that moment, swelling to a sudden crescendo in a tone of voice entirely unlike the calm and ponderous one he'd used a bit earlier, the President asked:

"In that case, why is it you prefer to live like savages fallen from the path of civilization, friends?"

How were we to answer a question like this? Was he suggesting we create a constitution, elect a grand assembly, and form a police force?

At the point he was convinced he had us thoroughly primed, he launched into a long diatribe.

"Look here, my dear neighbors," he said. "Humankind has struggled long and hard to attain today's level of civilization. For that cause, blood has been shed and heads have rolled, and no one among you today who calls himself a human being can afford to act in such a manner as to turn your backs on civilization and set back the human race. Since coming to this beautiful island, I've observed that there are a number of problems and mistakes in need of correction. It may be that you don't see them because you've grown so used to them, but when we correct these flaws together, everyone on the island will experience greater prosperity, peace, and wealth. What's at stake here are our common interests. None of us are rivals."

We still failed to understand what connection any of this had with the seagulls.

"Just think about it. The distinguished father of our friend Number 1 did all of you a major favor by allowing you to use his island and for each of you to build a house, never asking any payment in return. Never in my life have I heard of a nobler deed than this. Everything in this world is based on reciprocity. People are one before God, but in life they receive their lot in accordance with their intelligence, their abilities, their determination, and the strength of their desire to win. This is why there's no such thing as absolute equality. The fact is that the expression 'to give' isn't suited to human nature. No one ought to *give* anyone anything. Everyone ought to *earn*. Are there any among you who have read Ayn Rand?"

Here was another question being thrown at us for which our only answer was silence.

"Are there any among you who have heard of Ayn Rand's *Atlas Shrugged*, friends?"

"Yes," the Writer said, sounding bored. "I read it. Years ago."

"And yet," the President said, "I see that you've failed to grasp its message."

"It's not that I didn't understand it," was the Writer's quick retort. "There's a difference between comprehending and accepting. It's impossible for me to accept that woman's views."

The President laughed bitterly and retorted, "That's fine. Sooner or later, life will prove to you the truth of these views."

Unable to contain himself, Number 1 erupted into a loud fit of laughter. We all looked at him, and, a little embarrassed, he grew silent again. We were unable to make any sense of the sudden change in this man; it was as if he'd become someone else entirely since he'd started to pal around with the President.

A rueful committee member would explain it to us privately, in this way: The President had had his eye on Number 1 ever since the day he'd arrived on the island. "You're a chip off the ol' block!" he'd said to the island's heir, going on to have a chat with him that lasted for hours on end. "I'm very saddened by your situation," he'd said. "If he could see how you're doing, your father'd be saddened by it, too. Just look at the state you're in—you, the son of a distinguished and wealthy family! You're spending your life mixed up among the island's common folk. That's because they've inured you to their ideas of equality, to numbness, to not defending their rights. But don't forget, people aren't equal. There are the powerful and there are the weak, and life is a fight between the two. You ought to take your place among the powerful. In an age where tourism has progressed as far as it has and millions of dollars flow to the world's islands and coasts, is there any measuring what this island is worth? Tell me, is there? The islanders have duped you, made you think the diamond in your hand is a worthless bead. You're a wealthy owner and you ought to act accordingly. Equality, friendship, democracy: this is all a bunch of bullshit made up by the weak. They make it up because they need these kinds of notions in order to live. But the powerful have one desire and one desire alone: more power!"

It was clear that these words had made an impression on our friend, Number 1. He neither dressed like us nor acted like one of us anymore, and had begun to spend most of his time with the President.

Noticing the speech was growing long and meandering off in other directions, the Writer interjected: "If you'd please get around to the matter of the seagulls..." It gave the President an opening, and, bursting with emotion, he began to speak. He went on at length about how much harm the seagulls were doing to the island, how they frightened people, and about their attack that nearly crippled his poor granddaughter; how it would never do to hand over the island's beautiful coves to the seagulls. The seagulls were the enemies of everyone on the island. Which was why a war ought to be declared against them and why these creatures ought to be driven off the island for good. Because let's face it, civilization is, after all, about man's control of nature according to his wishes, is it not?

Frothing with excitement as he spoke and feeling no need to hide the seagull hatred within him, he went on giving the creatures a good dressing down even as they obliviously flew about overhead. He concluded his speech, infinitely convinced that he had the support of his so-called civilized neighbors on the issue.

The Writer was next to speak. With a weary voice, "We were," he began, "holding a committee meeting. These gentlemen said that it was necessary to destroy the seagulls on the island. I opposed it. When they forced the issue, I said that this is a decision of utmost importance, and therefore that we needed to consult with the rest of our neighbors. And now here we are before you. There's no need to go on at length; these ladies and gentlemen are planning to kill the seagulls on our island, break their eggs, and wipe them completely off the island. I don't suppose there's any need to say how insane this is. The seagulls were the ones who owned this island thousands of years ago, before we ever came; they've been laying their eggs and raising their young here for generations, teaching them to fly and hunt. The fact is, they do us no harm. I have trouble making sense of this merciless hostility toward the seagulls and the aim to destroy them. But I know, in any case, that you," as he glanced around the room at all of us denizens, "you who know what life on this island is like and who wish to keep from upsetting this state of harmony are not going to allow for this madness they're calling a 'mobilization against the seagulls.' That's why I have every confidence in the outcome of this business."

The room erupted with roaring applause. Our neighbors were shouting, "Bravo!" It appeared the President and his friends had met with defeat. And once our friend Number 32 got up and gave another similarly eloquent speech, the matter had become indefensible.

Clearly the islanders were opposed to this lunacy and there was nothing more that the President could do. Big grins had broken out across our faces, and not without having taken some pleasure in the man's defeat.

We were just about to leave when the President's wife stood up. She indicated for us to sit down with a wave of her hand. "My dear neighbors, there's something you've forgotten," she said. "This island belongs to someone. Namely, to the friend sitting beside us. You're all here by virtue of an act of generosity. While you may be the owners of your homes, the plots of land beneath them belong to Number 1. Which is to say, you have homes, but no land. Although Number 1 is very much a gentleman and would never go so far as to do something like this, the fact is, he could ask you to pick up your homes and leave at any minute. As the owner of the island, he has more of a right than anyone here not only to speak and be heard at this forum, but to make decisions concerning the island. He would be the first you should listen to, and I therefore suggest you do so."

Number 1 had been listening to all this with an air of embarrassment, his head cast downward. We noticed that he wasn't shocked by the things that had just been said, nor did he deny them. With a slight nod of his head, he even approved of them. Then he stood up. "My friends," he said. "You've known me for years; what's mine has been yours, and that's the way it'll always be. I have no intention of removing you from your homes, but you must admit that our dear elder, the respected statesman, has opened our eyes to a few matters of importance. Our President's ultimate intention is for everyone living on this island to become wealthier and more powerful. He is disappointed to see us living the shabby lives we've been living. Until the other day when he told me of his dream for the island, I, too, had been going about my life unaware of the island's incredible potential. But thanks to his ability to see the big picture, our President has broadened our horizons. He's presented us with new possibilities. With your permission, and at the expense of troubling him to do so, it is my wish that our President now share his dream with every one of you."

An awkward silence fell over the islanders. They then anxiously looked at one another. Despite the politeness in which the message had been couched, the fact was that they had just been told that the land on which they lived did not belong to them and that they could be thrown off of it by force of law. They had just been shown hell; a curious kind of heaven would be next.

The President stood up again.

"My dear neighbors," he began. "It is no small comfort to know that in addressing a distinguished crowd as intelligent and sophisticated as yourselves, there is no need to belabor the point. This is the Golden Age of world tourism. Each year, beautiful islands that lay claim to warm seas and blue coves are flooded by millions of tourists. Why doesn't our island, and by extension, why don't you, take part in your due of this wealth? There's nothing stopping us. The top firms of our country, and indeed of the world, can come here and start building five-star hotels, luxury casinos, discos, and entertainment centers as soon as tomorrow. You could all get your share of these millions of dollars. Yet instead, you've abandoned every one of this island's coves of heaven to the seagulls! Your heads having been filled with a bunch of cockamamie environmentalist notions— let the seagulls lay eggs here and whatever you do, don't disturb them—you've turned this paradise of an island into a garbage dump! Do you remember that word I mentioned to you from the very start, friends? That word 'civilization'? No civilized person would act this way, and no civilized person could possibly underestimate their personal interest to such an extent. So let's all take a vote now in favor of this measure and do away with this unnecessary seagull nonsense once and for all."

I looked around at the islanders sitting at the tables and saw that most of them had been jolted by these words. The poor islanders were in semi-shock: having just reckoned the whole business of opening war on the seagulls ridiculous, they were then threatened with being ousted from their homes, and now their heads were being filled with dreams of a life of riches. They didn't know what to believe anymore, and in fact, they couldn't think straight at all. It was as if they'd gone numb. Undoubtedly the result of any vote taken under these conditions would have been in favor of the President's wishes. The Writer must have sensed this, because he stood up and requested to speak again, but he was silenced by someone's explanation that he'd already used up his turn to speak. The group was ready to vote, though it was plain enough even now what the outcome would be.

Just then, a soft-spoken voice came from beside me. It was Lara, who with utmost politeness was requesting a turn to speak. "Look," she was saying, "the President's wife has spoken, but none of the women among us has been allowed a chance to speak yet. If civilization really matters so much to you, then it's only right you allow it."

Somewhat exasperated by this last obstacle that would add to the delay in taking the vote, the executive committee accepted it after exchanging glances with one another.

"Mr. President," Lara began. "When they came here today, all our neighbors were ready to object to your proposal. But now I see that they've begun to change their minds, given the way you've filled their hearts with hope with a promise of a life of milk and honey after threatening to kick them out of their homes. I congratulate you on your success in persuading them, but as a simple individual living on the island, I'd like to ask you something: How are you going to chase away the seagulls?"

"Who said anything about chasing them away?" the President said derisively. "We're going to annihilate them."

"How?"

"Haven't you ever seen a hunting party? We're going to hunt them all with shotguns. We're going to break their eggs, too. Think of it as a kind of hunting banquet."

"Given how determined you are on this point, couldn't we try to send the birds to the twin islands— without having to resort to such barbarism?"

Angered by her reference to barbarism, the President said, "OK, young lady. Do tell us then how it is we're going to send the birds to the other islands. Are we going to send them an announcement saying, 'Hey, birds! From now on, your place is on the islands across from here. Off you go!'?"

The fact that most laughed at this joke was a sign he'd won the case.

With a final effort, my sweetheart said, "We could put a bunch of fish on the islands and make shelters where they could keep their eggs. They'd take to it over time."

But the crowd didn't want to hear anything about a fish project of this sort. Objections rose from the crowd. "It's time to vote! Let's vote!" they were saying, and when the vote took place, most of our neighbors who had originally come to reject the proposal voted Yes.

All that was left to do now was to plan the slaughter. The seagulls, meanwhile, unaware of all these conversations, still screeched and shrieked as they flew about over the island, just as they had done for thousands of years.

Unable to look anyone in the eye, we left as soon as the meeting was over and retreated to our homes. Even though we didn't even want to think about the slaughter that was about to be planned, it was all that anyone could speak of.

If I were to use just one word to describe that night, it would probably be "shame." For the first time in the island's history, people felt shame in each other's presence and would avoid eye contact, even on occasions when they would run into each other on the street. At the end of that meeting, there'd been nothing left of our shared sense of being neighbors or friends. Everyone had taken off in a hurry, as if they wished to hide, the way guilty people do. There'd been neither the slightest of smiles nor a single nod of greeting, only frozen expressions and sullen faces.

And we had taken refuge in our homes.

Forever, and irretrievably, we sensed the kinship that we had shared had just vanished. This was the first major sign of the change to have taken over the island.

Ironically, the thing we had always cherished most about the island was that folks would spend most of their days together, in a way that made us feel like a family. It didn't matter that we saw each other every day; we'd still get to chatting up a storm whenever we'd see each other on the street or by the sea. We'd never run out of things to talk about, even though there may have been one or two individuals who were less inclined to join the daily chatter, being preoccupied with problems of their own. We had learned to pay them no mind, and just accept them as they were. Because our greatest unwritten rule was that no one was to interfere in anyone else's business.

That night, I quietly asked Lara, "What made you scold the President like that?"

"Because," she said, "I wanted to remind everyone once again of the savagery they're being dragged into. There isn't a single one of them who's in favor of violence, as far as I know, and we've known them for years. They're compassionate, easygoing, peaceful people."

"But circumstances change people."

"Even so, I doubt that these folks we've spent all these years with could turn into barbarians. When they get a look at the scene tomorrow they'll regret their decision and change their minds."

"You aren't upset with me, are you?"

"Why would I be?"

"You know I'm no good when it comes to talking in front of a crowd."

"Neither am I, but I felt that I had no choice."

My heart ached as I then remembered that a sense of having had no other choice had once motivated all the heroic victims of social uprisings with tragic endings. But Lara would be different. Nothing would happen to her, the way it had to them. I was determined to see to it that she remained safe from any harm that could arise from these kinds of matters from now on.

The island was buried in darkness, the houses dead silent. There was neither music nor laughter to be heard rising up from among the gardens. As the night wore on in all its oppressiveness, I caught even myself entertaining—or should I say, trying to entertain—thoughts of what our lives would be like if this were a touristic island.

Five-star hotels, airplanes landing and taking off from the sea, a marina full of anchored yachts, glittering hotel casinos, shapely girls in bikinis playing volleyball on beaches, young men surfing, an endless assortment of restaurants, job opportunities for everyone, wealth... How could the islanders possibly fail to be tempted by it all?

It seemed to me that this dream had most impressed folks whose children had made lives for themselves elsewhere, seeing as how no young person would have wanted to live on this remote and monotonous island. A touristic explosion could lead them all to come here and reunite with their families.

Throughout the night, listening to Lara's soft and rhythmic breaths as she slept, I went on imagining that other life. It was only later that the reasons became apparent, coming from someplace deep within me. And I must admit, I felt a little ashamed. I was doing it in order to avoid thinking about the Writer. Despite his urging me to speak out at the meeting against the slaughter that was about to take place, I hadn't. Instead, and to avoid meeting his eyes, I ran off as soon as the meeting was over. I knew damned well that he thought I deserved blame, and I was ashamed of my weakness. I couldn't see him. No, no—I simply couldn't see him. I didn't have the courage to look my dear friend and literature teacher in the eyes.

9

THERE MIGHT HAVE BEEN as many as a million birds in the sky. They would flap their wings, turning, swirling around one another, then break up again, flying in V-formation, suddenly turning around and amassing in chaotic flocks. These were birds that migrated to distant lands, traversing seas, plains, and countries. As they made their way across the ocean, they would reach a point over which they would fly amid one another in circles. The air was thick with the sound of chirping. It was a sound almost loud enough to fill the world. They were crying, shouting, demanding an explanation and lamenting desperately to each other.

"Where is the island?" they were asking. "Where is our island? We would always stop and rest at this island whenever we flew long distances, and our ancestors did too. But now our island is gone. Where are we going to land? Where are we going to alight? The island has disappeared. Under these conditions, there's no way we can go on. We won't make it to shore."

I was able to understand these conversations, without it seeming the least bit strange. In fact, I was surprised that I hadn't paid attention to the seagulls' conversations before then. It was as if I'd known their language for an eternity.

Thousands of chirping birds circled in jumbles in the sky, circling ceaselessly. They reached a point where they could no longer move their weary wings. They needed to find a bit of land on which to rest and gather their strength to complete their flight across the ocean, but the island they'd used as a resting point for thousands of years, etched into their genetic codes, had simply disappeared; it had, perhaps, sunk to the bottom of the ocean in an earthquake. They circled and circled, slowing down little by little, descending little by little, and then one among their midst, a silver-backed seagull, fell headlong toward the ocean. As the other birds looked on in shock, it splattered onto the glassy surface of the ocean—and died!

The others circled and shrieked some more, then another seagull struck its body on the ocean's surface, committing suicide. Then another, then another, then another!

By sundown, each and every one of the thousands of the birds circling the sky had ended its life. Bird carcasses floated on the waves, blanketing the surface of the ocean.

Then there was a deep silence. It was as though the world had ended.

BREATHLESS, it was then that I woke from the dream. Lara, who had draped an arm and a leg across my body, sensed my waking and asked, raising her head, "You look like you've just returned from the dead. Take it easy. Did you have a strange dream?"

"Yes!" I said, and told Lara about the dream, its every detail still as real as life itself. "Our island was gone," I said. "It had sunk to the bottom of the ocean, so the migrant birds were unable to find a place to alight as they crossed the sea, as they've done for thousands of years. They committed suicide, one by one, and the ocean swallowed them all."

Lara comforted me, stroking my head. "I seem to remember there being something like that," she said. "If I'm not mistaken, one of the old seamen saw that happen." Perhaps this bit of information had lodged in my subconscious. Perhaps it hadn't been a premonition about our island after all. We got up and went out to the yard, steeped heavily in the delicately sweet scent of jasmine; we drank a cup of chamomile tea. But nothing we did made a difference; we couldn't relax. We were terribly on edge in anticipation of the events of the next day.

The Writer was right, and I didn't want to even so much as speculate about what he'd meant when he'd said, "You ain't seen nothing yet!"

And now the nut harvesting season was here. These were days during which we should have been gathering nuts, instead of knocking ourselves out dealing with the paring of the trees into sculptures, border stipulations between houses, and enmity against seagulls.

Have I told you about that? Have I mentioned the pine nuts yet? I don't remember. But I think ... no, I don't think I have. I've told you, as a writer, this is as far as my skills go. I remember now that I failed to share this with you as I was describing our life on the island. I apparently skipped over this crucial detail right before the attack on the seagulls; my wanting to tell you about it now is awkward timing, but I've grown impatient to do so, because it's of consequence.

At any rate, let me briefly share this information with you: There is a fascinating genus of pine tree found on our island. A rare and precious variety of nut by the name of *Pinus pinea* grows on these trees. Because those nuts are worth a great deal of money, during this season we always climb these trees and gather up their pine cones, filling sacks with the nuts they contain. The sacks are left with the grocer, who sends them off with the next ferry. The merchants in the capital pay good money for them. It's the grocer again who receives the payment, distributing it evenly among the island's households. This money is enough to pay the small sum needed to cover the cost of our newspapers, milk, meat, etc. It is what constitutes the source of our modest living on the island.

That night Lara and I mused with some bitterness about the fact that this was the nut harvesting season, and had it not been for the trouble caused us by these events, right now we would be enjoying the happiness of the season. We felt miserable.

And yet what great times we'd had during those same days the previous year! The folks who had risen early would call out to their neighbors as they walked by their houses. Those who were able to catch up fell in step with the caravan and headed toward the forest. Everyone's hands were full with the day's lunch, refreshments, the sacks for holding the nuts, baskets, and more, and we'd carried them with great cheer. Those who hadn't been able to catch up would come later.

That kind of lateness was not a problem, because no one was counting how many hours each person worked or how many nuts each one of us had gathered. Everyone simply did as much as they could, or felt like doing. The ones who took the most breaks were our musician friends, and when they did, the sounds of flutes and guitars would fill the forest. As we would go about gathering the nuts, sometimes there would be a melody accompanying us to which we knew the words, and we'd accompany the musicians in turn. There were also times they would play music we'd never heard before, so I think they were improvising every once in a while. Yet their music was always comforting to us. There were times when they were less than eager to play music, politely turning down our requests by saying, "A little later." Birthdays and celebrations were another matter, however. They would come out and play from the heart on these occasions. And last year they'd played each and every one of our requests. When they didn't know how to play the song in question, they just made something up, and we'd laugh.

My attention returned to the present with the sound of Lara's voice. "We must stop this massacre!" she said. "We should warn our neighbors before it's too late." Then, despite the time being long past midnight, she sprang up with an energetic leap. "Come on," she said, "get up, let's go."

She grabbed me by the hand, dragging me behind her. Our first stop was the retired notary at Number 29. Intent on waking them up, once we got there we saw that no one was sleeping anyway. In fact, the residents of Number 30 and Number 27 were there as well, whispering among themselves in the garden.

When they saw us, we weren't surprised to see the look of delight on their faces, glowing in the light of the garden lamps. They were discussing the same subject, of course, wishing to stop this action from taking place.

Spoiling the peace on our island, the proposed killing was an undertaking that struck a raw nerve in us. We had been living side by side with those seagulls for years, and we'd grown used to each other. We had no problems with each other. The unprovoked murder of these innocent creatures and the destruction of their eggs was simply unacceptable. We absolutely had to stop this business from taking place.

The notary gentleman, who had a very temperate nature and whose opinion was much respected among the islanders, said: "I'm sure that most of our neighbors share our attitude. They wouldn't want to harm a single living creature, but today, they were at a loss for what to do. That decision was made despite their disagreement with it."

So we put our heads together and discussed what could be done at that hour. We could have convinced them to take preventive action, but it was late and the slaughter would begin in five or six hours.

We had a few moments of spontaneous silence, lost in thought.

I saw Lara get up and go into the house. She returned a few minutes later with a piece of paper in hand.

"I'm going to read you something!" she said. "Listen."

Then she read the following brief poem:

"The wind heeds no prohibition
Seagulls are not for locking up in chains
Any more than is one's heart."

I was baffled; I couldn't make any sense of her efforts with poetry when we were in the jaws of desperation.

Everyone must have thought the same, given the sudden silence among us. Unable to resist at this point, I said, "That's beautiful! Did you write this poem just now?"

"No, no!" she said. "You've got it wrong, it's not my poem, it's a poem by Pushkin that I've just changed around a bit, that's all! The actual one is about eagles."

The notary asked, "So what are we supposed to do with this poem?"

"We're going to write up a notice."

"What kind of a notice?"

"We're going to put this poem at the top, and underneath, we're going to add some lines expressing how crazy all this business is and prevail upon our neighbors not to go through with it."

"And then?"

"Then, within half an hour, we're going to slip this notice under everyone's door. We'll deliver them by hand to the people who are awake."

"That's my Lara!" I thought. Within her delicate, slender frame was hidden an extraordinary energy and fighting spirit. She wouldn't give in, driven to do all she could even with just hours to go before the slaughter was to get under way. That was my love! That was my soul mate! That was my one and only, my woman! My betrothed, who soothed the wounds of my soul with her words and wrapped the wounds of my body with her feminine powers.

"Come on, let's get going!" I said. "Let's make copies of the notices and pass them out to the houses. We can do it in an hour."

The notary gentleman and Number 27 expressed their doubts that the plan would work. And besides, those who had come to a decision had already come to one: What could a notice change at this late hour? And a *poem*, at that! A variation on a Pushkin poem; they didn't believe it would be of any use.

Exclaiming "The pen is mightier than the sword!" Lara ran into the house again, ignoring them, and began to write up a notice. I went beside her, read what she had written, and told her how much I liked it. I believed that the energy overflowing from her body would in itself be enough to convince everyone.

But things didn't turn out the way she had expected. The notary and his friends told us, after having thought matters over, they weren't willing to take the risk of stepping on residential premises at night when there were armed guards on the island. A plan of this nature might have worked in the past, but had we forgotten the incident at the President's house, not to mention the grocer's son, who got a beating? In an atmosphere as tense as this one, this could be a dangerous undertaking. People could get shot.

They proposed an alternative: it might work to wait along the road that led to the seagulls' cove early in the morning and hand out the notice there. Lara, an impatient soul, was less than satisfied with this approach, but at this point, there was nothing more to be done.

That night we slept fitfully, for no more than a couple of hours. Even sleeping in each other's arms was not enough to chase away the nerves that had consumed us.

At the first light of dawn, we ran to the road leading to the seagulls' cove. There was no one around. The white-hot sun had just begun to send out its bright rays of light over the ocean surface. The early birds were chirping among the trees. We felt a touch of coolness that energized us, making our bare shoulders shiver in the morning air.

We waited like that for a while, then stood up when we heard voices approach us. The President, his aides, Number 1, and Number 8 showed up one after the other, each with a shotgun in hand. The President, meanwhile, wore a pair of sunglasses, just like his aides. They were walking toward the seagulls' cove, ostensibly in high spirits.

They registered surprise when they saw us and tried to make sense of what we were doing there. They were perplexed as to the presence of Lara, who, of course, was there to oppose the slaughter of the seagulls. Had she changed her mind, or did she have some ulterior motive?

"Good morning!" the President said, smiling jovially. If anyone were unaware of the events up until now and of who this man was, one would have instantly concluded that standing before us was a cute old man who was simply saying good morning. Dressed in his white outfit, he looked quite handsome and clean-cut, the very image of discipline and refinement.

"Have you come to join us?" he asked. "Let's give you a shotgun each."

"No!" said Lara; "we aren't murderers!"

Upon which the President grew beet-red, quivering with anger.

"Watch your words, young lady!" he said. "Don't you forget who you're talking to."

Prompted by the President's anger, his aides moved toward Lara. I—with a courage I hadn't known I possessed—stepped in between them. I gave the notices in my hand to the aides, and then to the President and the others.

I could feel their surprise.

The President read it. "What is this?" he asked.

"A declaration of peace!" I said.

With as much astonishment as he had shown in the previous moments, the President read it aloud:

"'Dear neighbors. We have drawn up this notice to warn you about this morning's massacre of the seagulls. The island belongs to the peace-loving seagulls, and they are our neighbors. They settled on this island long before us and have made it their home for thousands of years. To murder these innocent creatures who do us no harm can only be explained by a lack of conscience and a bloodthirsty heart. We therefore call upon you dear, peace-loving islanders not to take part in this crime of humanity and to raise the flag of peace and well-being!'"

The President paused for a moment, then continued:

"The wind heeds no prohibition
Seagulls are not for locking up in chains
Any more than is one's heart."

For an instant he seemed dumbfounded at what he'd just read, then broke out into a fit of loud laughter. Not fake in the least, but genuine, unrestrained laughter that brought tears to his eyes. His guffaws spread to the others, who now were laughing too.

"And the poem! This poem!" he was saying as he choked on his guffaws. Through spasms of laughter, he tried to go on reading.

"Just listen to this: 'The wind heeds no prohibition' and...and...'seagulls are not for locking up in chains.' Have you ever read anything so stale, so unlikable, or so silly before? Have you? So then: 'Seagulls aren't for locking up in chains'!"

Number 1 said, "You'd think the poem was about Joan of Arc, not the seagulls, bless their little hearts!"

They exploded into laughter again. Meanwhile the President's aides, who were the only ones not to laugh, kept Lara and me under their careful watch.

I was overcome with anguish by my inability to do anything in the face of these taunts, of being unable to protect the girl beside me, but what could I have done, given that the men were armed!

After laughing some more, the President regained his composure and became serious. "I've seen a lot of these 'peace notice' tricks," he said. "All the subversives, terrorists, and anarchists who want to upset the social order hide behind these kinds of notices. My life has been spent putting them in their place. So now on this island too, these types have crossed my path, have they? Don't worry; everything's going to go just as it did in the past. Besides, no one buys these 'compassionate intellectual' pretensions anymore. Just look at this amateurish poem. Even an elementary school child wouldn't write a poem this bad. Leave it up to me and I'll write you fifty poems a day just like it. Hell, I could write a hundred of them!"

"It was written by Alexander Pushkin!" Lara said.

"There you go," said the President. "It's all starting to make more sense now. You've just admitted in your own words that you're part of a communist plot."

The President was slowly starting to forget that he was on the island; before we knew it he'd be giving his men orders to arrest the "subversive" before him.

"Alexander Pushkin," said Lara, "died years before the dawn of communism."

"Be that as it may," countered the President, "the Russians have always had a communist soul."

Then he suddenly turned to leave without so much as giving us another glance, and the others followed behind him. "Shame on you!" I whispered to Number 1 as he walked by me. "What you're doing is reprehensible!"

He hesitated for an instant, then turned without looking back, walking behind the President. This encounter was upsetting, but it actually shed light on a significant dimension of the situation that served to turn this defeat into a feeling of victory.

Then we realized we were alone. Despite the notices we held in our hands as we waited for those folks coming this way from the wooded road, no one was showing up. The place was silent. After waiting a while longer, the relief in us grew all the more, because still no one had come. Except for the President, his men, and two islanders. That was all!

We were filled with a sense of hope when we figured the islanders would not be taking part in this massacre. In the end, they had only assented to taking part in it because they felt they had no other choice, and probably came to their senses after thinking it over. The readiness in our hearts to believe in our islanders led us to see this silence as an act of popular resistance. We were proud of our neighbors. The one thing we couldn't explain was the ease with which Number 1 had fallen into the trap and become bedfellows with the President. Clearly enough, he was relishing the feeling of being the sole owner of the island and had begun to see himself as being above us. But at the rate things were going, we began to think we could win him back in the end.

We had just begun to savor the moment when we heard the first gunshot. We scrambled to the top of the adjacent hilltop from which the seagulls' cove could be seen. The sound of gunfire was intensifying.

We were met with a horrifying view once we arrived at the top. The President and his men were standing on the shore shooting at the seagulls, hitting great numbers of them, thanks to the expert professional marksmen among them. The seagulls were shrieking as they flew, leaving their eggs behind as they circled in the sky. We saw one or two of them hit the surface of the ocean, their bodies soaked with blood. They were falling from the sky just like the birds in my dream. The guns were going off one after the other. How frightening it was to have to watch this terrifying massacre. There was no stopping the tears flowing from Lara's eyes as she choked on her sobs and murmured, over and over again, "The filthy murderers! The filthy murderers!"

Though the gunshots must have been audible throughout the island, no one was around. Everyone must have gone home. I wondered what the Writer was doing, figuring that he, too, must have been watching the massacre from some other hilltop, or was sitting at home, blocking his ears, unable to bear witnessing the unfolding events.

The massacre lasted a few more hours, but there were so many seagulls that it would have been impossible to destroy them with a mere handful of shotguns. Though they could have escaped from the shore, they would return after flying off a short distance, entering the line of fire out of an instinct to protect their eggs.

After killing fifty or sixty seagulls, the men either had had enough, had grown tired, or were changing tactics. We saw them prepare to turn back.

Still shaking from shock when we got home, we heard the seagulls shriek ceaselessly in the sky. Some among them would no longer be able to return to the shore, or to their eggs that had once held their chicks.

10

I N THAT AGITATED STATE, we went out looking for our Writer friend. There was no longer
any need for us to feel ashamed in his company, as
we'd scored a victory, no matter how small. Some
seagulls had died, but the matter had ended, for the
most part, in a fiasco for the President and his men.
We assumed that, in light of the islanders' attitude,
they probably could not keep up with something
like this for long.

The Writer, however, whom we found sitting
and musing to himself on Purple Water, was of
another mind. He read the notice that Lara had

prepared, shook his head, and said that he liked it, but he saw no reason to be so optimistic.

He posited that the President wasn't someone to give up after a mere attempt or two. As far as he was concerned, whatever had taken place on the mainland, a smaller-scale version of the same was taking place here. Now that he was retired, the President had found himself a new, miniature-size country, and he was going to play with it to his heart's content. He would make use of the full extent of his experience and apply every last one of his dirty tricks.

"But the people..." I interjected into the Writer's assessment.

"What you call 'the people' is a fickle thing," the Writer retorted. "Today they act one way, tomorrow they act another. Depending on the threats and encouragements they're subjected to..."

Suddenly I had an idea that felt like the right thing to do.

"Look," I said, "let's go ahead with the pine nut harvest tomorrow. All the islanders can make a day of it. Let's have all our annual festivities as usual. Have dinner together after filling the sacks with nuts, just as we've always done; let's have our friends play folk dance music on guitars and flutes, and let's dance, just as before. Let's go back to our old lives, in other words. With all that excitement going on, the President will be all but forgotten, along with his damned mobilization for war. It's not as though he's going to come and say, 'Hey, let's go kill the seagulls!' while everyone's up in the pine-tree tops!"

I laughed then, particularly pleased with my words, but my suggestions fell by the wayside. The Writer and Lara did not appear to share my enthusiasm; in fact, they looked worried.

"I don't know...I have a terrible gut feeling about it, but let's go ahead and try it," Lara said.

The Writer agreed: "No way are we giving up the fight!" he said. "Of course we'll give it a try. But don't forget that it isn't going to be at all easy."

These were words I gave a lot of thought to later on. Sacrificing oneself when you knew the consequences full well must have been something on par with submitting to your fate. I had once read a sentence by Plato about wisdom: that when a wise man warns the people of impending rain but the people don't heed his warning, he isn't obliged to get wet along with the rest of the idiots, but has the right to retreat inside his home where he'll be dry and comfortable.

In the afternoon, we visited as many houses as we could, inviting our neighbors to come and take part in the nut harvest the next day. Maybe it was a week or two early, but the nuts had ripened and there was no reason not to pick them.

No word was heard from the President and his men the whole day. There was no trace of them. It was as if the island had gone back to its former days of tranquillity, preparing to harvest the pine nuts just as in years past.

That evening, the grocer's son distributed a notice to each of our houses. We knew something was wrong as soon as we saw the slip of paper. The notice was newly emphasizing the matter of who owned the island's property, stating that the pine nut trees were a part of that property and therefore that even a single nut picked from the pine trees would qualify as an act of theft. A photocopy of the deed to the island was also attached to the notice.

"A notice for a notice!" I remember thinking. "A title deed in answer to Pushkin!"

We were in the middle of dinner at the time, and the Writer was with us. Once we got past the initial shock, we thought about what to do. The Writer suggested that we not change our plans and that we go nut-picking the next morning at the agreed-upon time.

So, early the next morning with ropes and sacks in our hands, we took off for the nooks and crannies of that beautiful forest, its pine nut trees stretching up to the skies. There were about twenty of us. That meant that not all the islanders were joining us, but twenty was enough. To encourage the ones who were with us and attract the ones who weren't, we asked our island's guitar players and flute players to play music instead of gathering nuts. We'd gather the nuts for them too: it was our belief that the sight of us gathering nuts in high spirits would serve our cause. Grabbing their instruments, our friends joined us and began to play one lighthearted melody after another. On hearing the trilling of the flute, even the forest birds twittered along. As for the seagulls, they were nowhere to be seen; they weren't even flying, and we noticed the odd silence of their absence.

We went about gathering the pine cones and stuffing them into our sacks. We would later leave them to dry in the sun, breaking the pine cones to remove the tasty nuts within them after some time had passed, and ultimately package them. This was a practice we'd carried out for years. So it went, up until noon; we would manage to gather a good amount of pine cones, stopping for a break when the sun was directly overhead, then begin to eat the sandwiches we'd brought with us.

Just then, we saw the President's men make their appearance in the pine nut forest. They walked up and stood right in front of us and announced: "You're picking nuts on property that doesn't belong to you. This is a violation of the laws. Break it up now!" Though their sunglasses were hiding their stern gazes, their voices resonated with menace.

"We've been doing this for years. This place belongs to us all!" we said.

"That's not what the deed says, though," they said. "Break it up now!"

"We won't go without the say-so of the island's owner."

"It's on instruction from the island's owner that we're here."

"You don't have that authority!"

"We do. We're an attachment of the state security units, and this island is a part of our country. It is our responsibility to see to the execution of the law here. Break it up now, or else..."

"Or else what?"

At this point the men pulled out their shotguns and said:

"We have orders to arrest anyone who opposes this order."

The Writer laughed bitterly: "This island doesn't even have a jail!"

"You just try to resist. Then you'll see whether there's a jail or not," was their answer.

Things had gone too far. We had no choice but to stop our nut gathering.

With no other alternative, we took off, leaving behind the nuts we'd gathered. No one spoke on the way back. We all simply went home. The President had won. No one would be receiving their share of the island's sole source of income brought in by the nuts, and even worse, the men were so caught up in what they were doing that we could lose our houses.

On the one hand was the fear of destitution and losing our homes; on the other, the dream of great riches could now come only from the island's potential as a touristic paradise. An oppressive silence had settled over the island. Lara was too distressed to talk. Her belief that evil prevailed everywhere and that it inevitably defeated good had been confirmed all over again.

The notary gentleman and some of our friends had apparently tried as a last resort to visit Number 1. Placing their faith in the friendship they had once had with him, they went to ask him not to hurt his friends on the island, which he would do if he were to go along with the President. We didn't find out about this until later.

From what they said, Number 1 welcomed seeing them, beating around the bush at first, but then when they pushed the matter said, "Believe me, there's nothing I can do about this, either! It seems there are some legal conflicts in the deed to the island, and unless I go along with what the President says, it could be taken away from me. The island's inheritance and real estate taxes haven't been paid on time, resulting in an enormous amount that includes the interest that's been accumulating all these years. To make a long story short, the instant I protest, everyone including myself will have to leave the island. It'll go to the state. I'm sorry, my friends. We have no choice but to go along with what he says."

And then he began to defend the President: "Besides," he said, "he *is* the President, after all! It goes without saying that he knows better than we do how these things work. So hey, how about it—let's not get on the wrong side of the President just because of those bestial seagulls. If we all obey his instructions, we'll all steer clear of getting our noses bloodied and we'll all be comfortably well off. There's a lot of money to be had in the end too, no doubt about it!"

Our friends returned home, crestfallen and spiritless. As they told us of their meeting, with heavy defeat in their voices they said, "We aren't strong enough to fight the President! Best we simply follow his orders." We were filled with a sense of rebellion, tears streaming again from Lara's eyes, the Writer kicking at the stones, yet that was the bitter truth: there was nothing else for us to do.

That evening, another notice arrived at our houses. We were all being summoned to gather on the public square at eight in the morning in preparation to fight the seagulls. We had never imagined that we would one day receive orders to mobilize for war on this peaceful island of ours, yet that was exactly what we were facing at this moment.

The notice also stated that shotguns would be handed out to us, along with instructions for the men and women alike to be sure to wear pants and shoes. Since we wouldn't be returning home for some time, we could bring along water and, on the condition that it not be an excessive amount, a parcel of food. Wearing hats and sunglasses was also suggested.

At night in bed, Lara cried silently, her tears once again dampening my cheeks. Then, in a voice of utter hopelessness, she suggested we leave the island. "Let's get out of here!" she said. "This isn't an island. It's a concentration camp!"

"But where can we go?" I said. "It's a concentration camp everywhere. Besides, while it's the seagulls that are being killed here, it's people that are being killed over there. Do you actually think that the conditions in the city we came from are any better than here?"

Lara didn't answer, her shoulders continuing to shake. My heart was breaking, but there was nothing I could do.

11

HOW STRANGE! Though it had been with the seagulls that the conflict had begun, it was as if things were growing more personal and turning into a fight among us humans. Yet as bitter as it may be, this much I must admit: this fight had brought a certain liveliness to the island. Perhaps the excitement of the fight was something our convoluted souls had long been wishing for. I could see as much in Lara's face as it reddened with exasperation, her cheekbones turning bright pink, and at times in the festering hatred in my writer friend's eyes.

How were the seagulls faring while all this was going on among the humans? What were they doing? How were they tending to their wounds? There was no way for us to know, not only because we had had no time to watch them, but also because their blank and dignified expressions made it all but impossible to tell.

Before the unfolding of these events, I had sometimes wished I could have put myself in the seagulls' position and watched the island from their point of view. While we humans went on walking, talking, and eating as they looked down on us from the sky, how did they see us, I wondered? What did they think about us?

We humans think about the universe and arrive at various conclusions, but we never wonder what the universe thinks about us.

But none of these thoughts were of any use to us now. It was morning; the sun had begun to bathe the island in its glow, its light reflected like a mirror across the surface of the sea. The leaves looked even more vibrantly green with the dew that had fallen overnight. As the morning fog faded away, we made our way toward the pier in a state of suspense. The first to appear were the President's men who lived in the boat, followed by Number 1. Then, one by one, a few of our neighbors arrived on the scene. The President wasn't there yet. They were probably waiting for the crowd to assemble before calling him. That's the way it had to be done, as per the laws of the state, for all we knew!

We counted the number of islanders to show up: eighteen. None followed later, and even the ones who *had* shown up were nervously looking around, as if on the alert for the first chance to escape.

The President then made his appearance. We watched him give them a long speech. His men gave out shotguns to everyone. Then they began to walk, the men in dark sunglasses out in front of them, and the President just behind them. The islanders watched them like a terror-stricken army detachment. We began to follow them from a distance.

Just as I was looking up at two seagulls flying overhead, I heard the Writer's voice. He had planted himself before the detachment on the road running beneath the clean-shaven treetops and was shouting at the top of his lungs: "Stop! Stop! I won't allow you to take a step beyond this point!" The President, shocked to be confronted with such inconceivable audacity, asked, "Who the hell are you?"

"As an islander, I hereby oppose this massacre!"

"Move aside, or I'll have my men put you in a world of pain!"

"I'm not moving. I won't allow you to slaughter the seagulls."

"Why the hell should the seagulls be of any concern to you? And don't you see—the island's owner is with us, too."

"The real owners of this island are the seagulls. They got here thousands of years before we did!"

"But they're savages. How could savages possibly own an island?"

"So they're savages—and you think you're civilized?"

"Of course I am. Only the civilized can own property. It makes no difference how long the savages have been living here. The fact is, they don't own the island."

"The seagulls are the owners of this island!"

"No, sir. The seagulls are this island's enemy." Turning to his henchmen, the President barked, "Get this jerk out of my way."

On this heated command by the President, two of his men, chomping at the bit as they'd stood by him during this exchange, walked toward the Writer and, swatting his head with the butt of a shotgun, dragged him to the side of the road. The Writer must have lost consciousness, because he wasn't moving. Without a clue about what to do, I began to bite my tongue in my nervousness, at the same time keeping a tight grip on Lara after she'd lunged forward, in an attempt to prevent her from doing something as crazy as running to the Writer's side. If I had let her go, there was no doubt she would have been next to receive the same blow to the head.

Then we heard the President say to his men, "Take this subversive and lock him up somewhere!" They grabbed the Writer by each of his arms and dragged him away. The President and the rest of the crowd dispersed.

After following them, we were unfortunate enough to witness a massacre even worse than the one we'd seen the day before. Again the seagulls shrieked as they flew. They would leave their eggs behind, only to fly back out of instinct, get hit with bullets, and drop, blood-soaked, into the sea. Their feathers swirling in the air after them, they would fall into the water like burst and swollen red balls.

Their efforts to protect their offspring were spurring on their killers to act with even greater violence. It brought tears to one's eyes. The islanders were being more cautious, and it was obvious that they were taking no pleasure in what they were doing, since most of them missed the shots they took. But the President and his men went on shooting, proudly pointing out the birds they would hit. They kept it up until they arrived at the cove, where they began to crush a few of the eggs beneath their heels. We couldn't see them from where we were standing, but we could only imagine the horrific sight of the eggs of the seagulls being smashed beneath the men's heels. The seagulls, having all but gone mad, began to attack those on shore, in a swift swoop down on them, but they were left helpless against the shotguns. The men went on killing and the seagulls went on dying.

A mass of seagulls appeared on the surface of the sea. But this sight was not the same mass of white amid the blue sea that I'd seen in my dream. Their necks broken, their wings smashed, they rocked on the gentle waves of a bloodred sea.

The cries of seagulls rang out through the air. These weren't like their usual cries. It wasn't the same sound of the seagulls that we'd grown so used to, living on the island for all those years. It was a cry, an absolutely heart-wrenching expression of terror that we were hearing for the first time. Lara was beside me, shuddering violently as she cursed the men and wept.

On the days when there were waves at sea, the two of us would sit on the shore, unable to get our fill of watching the fledgling seagulls as they rocked on the waves. The seagulls were like babies, and we loved the way they would climb aboard the swelling waves and surrender to their rise and fall, as if rocking in a cradle. The black dot just behind their eyes made it seem as though they had an extra pair of eyes. Our hearts would fill with tenderness at the sight of that wobbly, vulnerable way of standing that the young among all living creatures have.

At one point, I noticed the grocer's son on the shore, off by himself, quite a distance from the rest of the group. I saw him occasionally squat down, then stand up. I was unable to see exactly what he was doing, but it seemed to me that he must have been breaking the eggs too. What was he up to? Maybe he was going along with everyone else and smashing the chicks, unaware of what he was doing.

A while later, I was surprised to notice that the seagulls had disappeared from the island. It was as if they'd arrived at a collective decision, or received an order, and changed direction. Having given up flying back to their eggs, they flew off toward the south of the island. Because the area was cut off by a cliff, they suddenly disappeared from sight. At this point there wasn't a single seagull in sight; nor was there any sound of their cries. An absolute silence had settled over the island.

Faced with this silence, the President and his men could find nothing to do but lower their shotguns and, with a savage joy, begin to trample on the eggs. Raising their feet, they would stomp as hard as they could. The eggs crunched and crackled. We could even hear the sound from here. The islanders, still there against their will, weren't stepping on a single egg.

There was nothing left for us to do there anymore. We took off in an attempt to find out where they'd locked up the Writer. Lara had an idea en route. Her voice hoarse from crying, she said, "Let's go see this tyrant's wife! Let's tell her about the massacre. She *is* a woman, after all. She's got children, grandchildren. If we appeal to her conscience, she may make a bid to persuade her husband not to go on with it."

That was the way Lara was: never surrendering, making every effort to grab on to some new ray of hope even in the most hopeless moments. And she was right, because despite all the slaughter that had already taken place, the President and his men had managed to do harm only to just a few of the thousands of seagulls spread out over the island's banks. If we could stop the massacre now, we'd have achieved a significant victory.

We were greeted at the door by the annoying granddaughter again. A tall adolescent, the girl looked us islanders over with vast contempt, feeling no need to hide her attitude even as we came face-to-face. It was no different when she opened the door that day. "What do you want?" she asked in a la-di-da tone, her eyebrows arching. She came off like a shrewish princess deigning to meet her subjects' eyes. "Damn you!" I thought. Then I asked to see the President's wife.

The girl was saying we couldn't just stop by their house whenever we felt like it, when I heard Lara roar like an angry lion. "Go tell her that we've come—*now*! Immediately!"

The girl was taken aback by this outburst. She hesitated for a moment, as if unsure of what to do, her face puckering up as though about to cry, then she went inside. I was grateful she didn't slam the door in our faces.

A short while later the President's plump wife came in, all smiles. "Come in!" she said. "Come in, folks! How about a cup of coffee?"

Surprised at this positive reception, we looked at each other, then stepped inside, sitting down on the seats to which we were shown. Unlike the other houses on the island, this one wasn't sparsely furnished, but was decorated almost like a city house. Chairs in floral upholstery, polished coffee tables, floor lamps, paintings; the atmosphere of this house was nothing at all like that of the others.

Turning down the offer of coffee extended by the President's wife, Lara said, "Ma'am, do you know how pelicans feed their young?"

"No!" said the woman, dumbfounded.

"The mother pelican, rather than see her young go hungry, feeds them flesh she tears from her own body."

"Really? How interesting! I didn't know that. Makes for quite an impression!"

"Ma'am, if a pelican feeding her young were killed, how would you feel?"

"It would be a shame, no doubt about it—though, I must say, I don't see what you're getting at... To what do I owe this visit, miss?"

"Just as with the pelicans, the seagulls want to protect their young, and yet they're being massacred as we speak. The mother and father seagulls are being killed with bullets, while the baby seagulls are being stomped to death beneath boot heels. Please, ma'am, I implore you! Speak with your husband and tell him to put a stop to this brutality."

As Lara spoke these words, I noticed that the President's wife first froze before averting her gaze in an attempt to put a distance between us. She was staring at a fixed point beyond the window, her thin lips pursed.

"You're a mother too," Lara continued, "as well as a grandmother, ma'am. Were you to see such brutality, you'd be unable to bear it. Were you to see how the poor seagulls screech and cry in an effort to protect their children..."

"That's enough!" the President's wife spat out, standing up. At which point we felt obliged to stand up along with her.

"Do you have any idea how many times in my life I've heard pleas just like this?" queried the President's wife with sudden indignation. "What's more, that they weren't made on behalf of birds, but people?"

Though she paused for a moment here, it was of course impossible for us to have answered such a question. She continued:

"The spouses and mothers of the arrested, the families of those condemned to execution, women searching for their lost children—which is to say, one go-between after another."

"And what did you say to them, ma'am?"

"I always gave them the same answer: My husband is a statesman and I never interfere with his business. He's the one who knows what to do where affairs of the state are concerned, while I tend to affairs of the home."

"But he's not in charge of a state now," I said.

The woman snapped. "There's no such thing as a minor position when it comes to government! Since my husband is the governing head of this island."

"But you're the President's assistant!" Lara said. "You should have some authority, too. Besides, sometimes women have a better sense of what to do than men."

These last words had obviously flattered her. Her face softened a little. "My girl," she said, "there's a limit to what I'm able to do. That's the way it's been all these years. I don't want to disappoint you, but you must believe me when I say that I simply don't get involved in these matters."

Clearly the woman wasn't going to be of any use. With no other choice, we headed toward the door. Slipping past the girl, who gave us a malicious look as she held the door open, we stepped outside. But just then, Lara said to the President's wife, "Then at least help us secure the release of our Writer friend who was arrested this morning. Surely you won't withhold a kindness as small as this from your neighbors."

I think the word "neighbor" made an impact on the woman, as if it could be a reminder that she'd have to go on facing us, and of the need to be a little better about the way she treated the people she might be spending the rest of her life with.

"All right," she said, a fake smile glued to her face. "I'm not promising anything, but I'll go ahead and have a talk with him."

Once outside, I asked Lara, "How on earth did you think of pelicans?"

"I don't know," she said. "When I was thinking of how to start off in a way that would make an impact with the woman, somehow it was the pelicans that suddenly came to mind."

"Do they really feed their young their own flesh?"

"I don't know. Plenty of people think so. Since ancient times it's been a widely held belief. In fact, they compare the pelican to Jesus Christ for the way he had the sins of humanity forgiven with his own flesh and blood.

"But even this didn't convince the woman!"

"Truly! What calloused hearts these people have!"

"If you ask me, I don't think the President can go for very long without killing people. He's grown used to it over the years."

"He must feel useless when he goes without killing."

"Who knows. The human heart is so dark, so complicated."

Walking toward the pier as we spoke, we heard the sound of music being played in the distance. We were suddenly quiet. The sound, coming in waves through the breeze, seemed to be seeping into our consciousness not through our ears, but through our hearts. Though it wasn't loud, it managed to reverberate vividly inside our heads. It had such an effect on us that it left us feeling just as we had in the midst of the seagull massacre. It was as if the air were once again being pierced by the shrieks of seagulls. A bit farther down the road, we saw a small crowd gathered around a house, listening to the musicians play their flutes and guitars.

We'd grown used to the way these friends of ours would convey calm and contentment through their instruments, sometimes accompanied by a cheer. Our peaceful days on the island had also included times when the melodies were quite melancholy. Separations, sorrows, and bitter memories weren't exactly unfamiliar to us as the years came and went and we grew older, amid emotions that couldn't always be expressed through words. There were even rare times when dirges were played. That evening, though, was the first time we were hearing a heartrending scream in the midst of the music.

As we walked on past the small crowd gathered in front of the house, the melodies still streaming in our wake, I heard the sound of Lara's voice. She was cursing the President and his men, sobbing all the while.

The beauty of the island had turned into a source of trepidation that made my heart ache. I felt helpless. "I remembered that you'd told us of all of these things in earlier days," I thought of saying to the Writer, "that you had warned all of us, and I felt something inside me break. In a way that could never be repaired."

We humans, in spite of not knowing our limits, are partial to our own beliefs; we don't learn, we don't grow wiser. And by the time we do, it's usually too late. The ache settling into my heart that afternoon as we set off in search of you, trying to find out where they'd locked you up, was like an ominous premonition telling me that matters were only to get worse.

What can I say—forgive me!

I don't know whether you're alive, whether you're at the bottom of a sea choked with seaweed, or whether you're six feet underground.

Even if you're alive, there's no way for you to hear these words I'm writing, yet I want to call out to you all the same, my dear friend.

Forgive me!

Forgive me!

Forgive me!

12

A T THE END of that melancholy day, we were sitting glumly in our garden, sipping our wine in sorrow amid the scent of geraniums, feeling that the night was our protective shelter. I kept thinking, "Why is this man so evil?"—over and over.

The Writer was with us as well, having been released from the woodshed behind the grocery with the efforts of the President's wife that afternoon. He had earned the distinction of becoming the first person on the island to be arrested. Though he never spoke of his past, we suspected that this wasn't the first time something of this nature had happened to him. "I've managed to get arrested even here," he said, smiling bitterly. His head must have been throbbing like crazy from the blow of the shotgun butt, because he'd asked for a painkiller as soon as we got home.

Lara asked the same question that had been going through my mind a short while earlier, but almost as if she were talking to herself. These types of coincidences had been taking place on a frequent basis lately. It must have been some peculiar form of telepathy that had come about from living together.

After saying nothing for a moment, she murmured again:

"Why is this man so evil?"

None of us said a word. The night was still, with no sound of the seagulls' cries, the island deathly silent. Could it have been possible that the President was successful in carrying out his plan and had driven all the seagulls from the island? Why hadn't we seen a single seagull in flight that afternoon or evening? Where had they gone? We'd never spent a day on the island without seeing the seagulls, or hearing their cries, and for us, that made the silence surrounding us a frightening one. It was as though we were on a foreign planet rather than on the same island we'd always known.

After taking another sip from his wine, the Writer broke the silence.

"This man is scared out of his wits, and there's your explanation for his evil: the immense fear inside him! The murders he's committed are going to haunt him for the rest of his life, descending on him like a curse. Even on this distant island he's escaped to."

Revealing again her fondness for poetry, Lara then said, "The rabbit doesn't run away because it's scared; it gets scared because it runs away!"

The Writer and Lara seemed to be lost in conversation. As for myself, I was thinking that these two people whom I so loved would never be able to make any sense of humankind's tendency to violence, because they could never feel it in their hearts. To me, the matter was simple. In this world there were two kinds of people—those who were good and those who were bad. I couldn't say what it was in relation to that they were good or bad, but there it was all the same. It was clear to me. Meanwhile, as far as I could make out, Lara and the Writer were lost deeper in conversation than ever. I tried to step in every once in a while to express my thoughts on the matter, but they went on talking without paying much attention to me.

The Writer told us what he knew about the President. As he spoke, I looked alternately at him, then at Lara's pallid face in an effort to make out what she was thinking. The President had grown up in a poor family, his father a religious clerk. As with most children of the populace, he had been registered at a free military school. According to the Writer, here the President had been brainwashed and taught that our nation was surrounded by domestic and foreign enemies alike, and that the duty of protecting it had been given to the military alone. They then set out looking for traitors. After finishing school, the President had married, had children, and taken a low-paying government job in one of the country's troubled areas. On reaching higher ranks, however, fortune had smiled upon him, a wave of nationalistic fervor making it possible for him to rise to the position of state minister.

"And the upset in the balance of the nation coincides with this period, as it happens!"

As the Writer nodded his head in approval of these words, I once again found myself admiring Lara's logical acumen.

"Yes, he had the sort of mentality where running the country means pitting political, ethnic, and religious groups against one another. He saw this as being the epitome of politics."

The truth is that I didn't really know much about these things. You couldn't exactly say that I took an interest in politics back when I was living on the mainland. I knew about the contentious election, protest demonstrations, the state of political disquiet, the arrests, the military trucks roaming the capital's streets, but I didn't have the foggiest notion about the magnitude or causes of the matter. The official notices broadcast on the radio and TV had frightened us all, making us believe that we were facing great danger. I'm ashamed to say it now, but the claims of arrests, torture, and death gave us the sense that maybe their opponents deserved it.

At long last I asked the Writer the question burning inside me: "Were you arrested too, during this man's rule?"

A shadow crept across his face, his voice growing hoarse, as he muttered under his breath something that sounded like, "That's another matter."

Lara shot me a look that told me to keep quiet, so I did. No matter how hard we tried, there was just no getting the Writer to talk about his past.

He'd erected a wall at a point in his psyche that no one could go through. You could get to this point, and never any further.

As the two of them went on talking, I came to realize that my brain didn't work the same way as Lara's, nor as the Writer's. I tended to focus more on the matter of the good and evil within people and would try to pull the discussion in that direction. A book I read years ago kept coming to mind.

"Each of us is, in fact, an alligator!"

They looked at me in astonishment. "Carl Sagan," I interjected, "believed in something called the R-factor. The letter R stands for the word 'reptile.' The R-factor says that because humankind came into being emerging from water onto land, there are still traces of reptilian violence at the root of our brains, and that we are predisposed to violence for the purpose of protecting our territory. In other words, we're all alligators."

At last, I'd managed to direct their attention to this point, now that the Writer had begun to speak of the good and bad within humankind as well. He mentioned Jean-Jacques Rousseau's *Emile*, and the articles Freud had written about humankind's destructive tendencies.

He explained the subject of "nature versus nurture" to us at great length. Are people born evil or are they taught to be evil?

"These are all just individual theories," he explained. "I don't think they're enough to settle the issue."

We spoke for a while about our neighbors on the island. We had mixed feelings on this matter, really. It was clear that there was a group, though small, who were unable to resist the President's threats and had taken sides with him, participating unwillingly in the massacre. They hadn't shot at the seagulls, hadn't broken the eggs, but had only shown up at the site for the sake of appearances. This was in contrast to most of the islanders, who had ignored these threats and hadn't taken part in the massacre.

I mentioned something else I'd heard late that afternoon. The President had called the musicians to the scene and asked them to play melodies to support the fight against the seagulls, as well as get people excited about the cause. But none of them had accepted this ridiculous proposal. Our musician friends played music that had such a purity and natural quality about it that you would often forget that it was music at all, believing instead that it was one of the natural sounds of the island. It was a part of our lives. Some evenings it was as though the sounds of the guitar and flute had been echoing on the island for as long as it had existed.

As this conversation went on through the night, surrounded by the stillness of the island, the sweetly scented lemon balms continued to spray their intoxicating sap, while the ever more powerful scent of geraniums permeated the air, virtually transforming where we were sitting into a magic garden. Something I never forgot, never once put out of my mind, even as the heated discussion went on, was the heart-wrenching love I felt for Lara. I loved her so much that I ached.

And indeed, my heart was truly aching at that moment. It made it seem as though no matter how serious and heavy the subject matter, everything we spoke about was trivial. I felt like I lived only to see her face and hear her voice. Were they beautiful? Sure, they were beautiful, but what an insignificant detail this was, in my eyes. Were something to happen to her, her face to change, or even to grow ugly, I wouldn't have noticed. What captivated me about her was something far different from beauty. It was something ineffable: a certain air about her, a certain attitude, a delicate crack in her voice, a barely noticeable shadow across the edge of her lips, the tiny dent that formed on her chin when she laughed...all of these things, each and every one of them, were beautiful, but what mattered even more was that each of us was a twin soul to the other. This was our shelter, the kind in which you remain for a lifetime, and the kind that brims with the exquisite delight of every moment.

Our long conversation ended with Lara's words on Far Eastern beliefs: that each negative event experienced by a person leads to a closing of the person's chakra, which in turn results in a spread of negative energy. And there you had the reason for the man's evil. The Writer frowned, indicating that he wasn't exactly pleased with our particular interpretations of the matter.

"Then obviously the guy doesn't have a chakra left in his body," he said. "They're all clogged up." Then, as if he were giving a lecture, he said: "Look, you don't understand the heart of the problem, which is this: these men are afraid of just one thing, and that thing is a question. It frightens the hell out of them when any questions are asked. And as for those who question the system, they keep up their resistance out of a sense of necessity, even at the risk of self-destruction. Just like Jesus Christ, or Spartacus, or many other examples throughout history. So please don't go chalking the matter up to the goodness or evil of individuals!"

"Your point is well taken, but then why is he killing the seagulls? It's not as though *they're* questioning the system!"

The Writer hesitated for a moment, confused, uncertain of how to answer. Half-joking, he said, "Maybe you're right. Ah! Don't get me started!" Then, murmuring, "Besides, wherever there's evil, everyone there is partly to blame for it," he got up and tottered home. From the way he was holding his hands to his head, it was evident that his head still ached.

Both the shotgun-butt blow to his head and the hours he'd spent in the woodshed must have stirred up terrifying memories for him, making it impossible to keep his temper in check, and we could sense from the tone of his voice that he was even a little angry with us. It used to be that he'd only get irritated with me over some issue involving literature. To the tune of: "Is your name Proust? Is your name Borges?" whenever he would catch me imitating some famous writer's style. But we were in no state to talk about such matters now.

After the Writer had gone, the two of us carried on with the discussion for another five or ten minutes and then finished our wine. Before going to bed, I told Lara the story of the sparrow and the hunter, meanwhile bemoaning the fact that I hadn't thought to tell it earlier, because the Writer liked such stories, too. According to this story—told to me when I was a child—there was once a sparrow who alighted on a tree branch with her young in the middle of winter. By and by, they saw a hunter approach them, his mustache frozen, his eyes brimming with tears from the cold. "Look, Ma!" the baby sparrow said. "What a compassionate man he is! His eyes are full of tears." After warning her young one to be quiet, the mother sparrow then said, "Never mind the tears in his eyes. It's the blood on his hands you should be looking at!"

Lara loved the story. Not only were we in the position of the sparrow, but we also knew how to deal with the hunter. We made our way to our bed through the garden's intoxicatingly sweet fragrances, and began again to make love in our own way that healed us, a soothing balm on our wounds. The way she took me into her, her acceptance of me into her delicate body like a coy princess, was like taking refuge in the rejuvenation and life-saving mercy of a lake in the desert—a lake that you've discovered is real and not a mirage! At the end of our long and blissful love-making, and just before nodding off to sleep, I know very well what I felt.

Gratitude!

I was full of gratitude for her: a gratitude so deep that every now and then it would bring hot tears to my eyes.

13

THAT NIGHT in the hours just before sunrise, the island witnessed the first mass assault by seagulls in its history. We had yet to discover this as we sprang out of bed, panic-stricken in our belief that a bomb had gone off inside the house. Still half-asleep, we ran to our living room in the direction the noise had come from, the fresh, cool air of morning hitting our faces. The windows were broken. We turned on the light. We saw a seagull lying blood-soaked in the middle of the room. It was quivering and in pain, on the verge of death. It died quickly, stiffening as its head fell to the side. The appearance of the blood-drenched dead seagull was ghastly. We'd seen the dead seagulls on the sea, and before that, the ones that had died along the shore, but this was something completely different, because it was inside our house. It was lying just in front of the couch.

Lara was quivering beside me. As we began to get over our initial shock, we noticed the clamor and shrieks coming from outside. Glass shattered, the clay tiles on the roofs broke, and flocks of seagulls screeched.

Daring to poke my head out past the broken window, I saw what seemed to be all the seagulls in the world, gathered on our island. It was as if they weren't flying, but rather flowing, from one location to another as a single mass, turning the dark dawn's sky to white. Their shrieks nearly deafened us. We heard shouts rising up from the houses. Then there was a clattering on our roof as well, as if someone had climbed up there and was breaking the tiles.

We would realize the next day that this, too, was part of the seagulls' assault. They had picked up large stones from the cove, which they were now dropping on the roofs of the houses. Gathering speed on their way down, they would smash the roof tiles like bullets.

Though we had read that seagulls were an extremely intelligent species capable of organizing, when we noticed that some had initiated the breaking of roof tiles, while others had taken on attacking the humans, and still others launching kamikaze-style suicide attacks, we couldn't believe what we were seeing any more than we could believe what we were hearing.

They were carrying out a systematic, well-planned attack against the islanders and the houses they lived in, in a way that required thought and sacrifice. Some of the seagulls were swooping down on the houses from great heights, hurling themselves against the windows at inconceivable speeds. The resulting collision made for an effect like that of a bomb, the seagulls' speedy death trajectory causing the windows of the house to explode. The gunfire we'd heard at the onset of the seagulls' attack had stopped in the meantime.

By the time morning had arrived, we were afraid to go outside. Because we couldn't have remained under those conditions forever, after much effort I got Lara to agree to stay at home while I made a bid to stick my nose outside. I had gotten no farther than the garden gate before the seagulls appeared full of wrath overhead. As they began to strike at my head, it was everything I could do throw myself back inside the house, trying to protect myself with my hands.

That day, we were able neither to go out nor to make contact with anyone. Every once in a while I would peek around a hidden corner to try to make out what was going on. The seagulls' raid continued intermittently. We tried to cover the broken windows by nailing curtains over their frames, securing the others as much as possible with fabric and furniture. Then we took shelter in our room.

What was happening to us had taken us by such surprise that we couldn't think straight. But we were well aware of one thing: it never occurred to us to be angry with the seagulls. On the contrary, the hatred we felt toward the President had only increased for causing all of this in the first place. What was he doing during the attack, we wondered? What was he thinking?

So the day went on like this, the seagulls never allowing us to go outside. It was no different than if bomber airplanes were flying over the island, as if an air raid had been launched against us.

The next morning, a dense fog settled over the island. It was white as milk outside, the mist so thick you couldn't see your own hands in front of your face except for a few indistinct figures. This was one of those foggy days that would transform the island into a fairy-tale world; never before had the fog pleased us as much as it did that day.

Lara and I cautiously stepped outside and began to walk around, keeping our guard up. There were no seagulls in sight, but then again, you never knew. If they were to assemble overhead, we'd be defenseless. First we went to the notary's house, where we also found the Writer, his musician friends, and some of our other neighbors. Their windows had been shattered too; their houses, ravaged as if by war.

As could be expected, a significant portion of our meeting was spent cursing the President; he'd done nothing but ruin the island by coming here with his ridiculous ideas. The seagulls weren't in the least to blame here. What was he going to do now, we wondered? The right thing would be for him to leave the island, to pack up and disappear along with his hateful grandchildren and that heartless wife. We got so angry that we fueled one another's fire to such an extreme that we were overcome with the need to say it to his face. The Writer felt likewise, and he would be the one to relay our thoughts to the President. He had unwittingly become our spokesman.

Together we set off in the direction of the President's house. The fog was so thick that it seemed as though all the clouds in the sky had descended on the island and were drifting at ground level. When I waved my hand, I caused a swirling in the mist. A few more of our neighbors joined us along the way. The members of the island community were finding each other and pulling together automatically. Everyone was furious with the President.

When we arrived in front of the President's house, the first thing that struck me were the armed men waiting on the veranda. The sullen-looking men were standing guard with shotguns in hand, but we were so enraged by this point that we were unfazed.

Speaking in unison, we said we wanted to see the President: "Tell him to get out here—right now!" When the men hesitated, appearing reluctant, we responded more forcefully than before: "Immediately!"

The President showed up on the veranda a short while later. I couldn't tell whether his face had grown pale or it only seemed that way to me, but it was obvious that he was considerably shaken up.

"Well, there you have it," he said. "Now you've seen just what dangerous creatures the seagulls

are, haven't you, my dear neighbors? You kept ignoring me even as I tried to warn you of that fact.
You were defending these savage creatures against
me. Tell me, just how are they any different from
terrorists, huh? Just how?"

"Do you have no shame at all?" blurted out the
Writer. "Where do you get the guts to say such
things? Don't you see what you're doing, don't you
see what's become of the island, the state you've put
us in?"

The Writer was having a fit, on the verge of a
nervous breakdown, saying, "Don't you? Don't you?
Don't you?!" over and over again. We backed him
up, wagging our hands at the President as we looked
at him in anger. His men seemed slightly confused
and surprised. They appeared to be having doubts
for the first time since coming to the island.

I felt particularly proud of the Writer for the
way he'd defied and nearly managed to scare the
President that morning. He stood there fearlessly
facing the President and his men, demanding that
they give him an account of their actions.

"What, you're blaming *me* now?" said the President, though he sounded less forceful than before. "Am I the one who broke all the windows,
all the tiles on the roofs? Am I the living bomb

that attacked your houses? Was I the one to force you to stay indoors? Please! Let's get real here! We should be putting our heads together to figure out how to save ourselves from this disaster, not blaming each other!"

"It is not civilized behavior to kill the young of birds!" the Writer cried. "Attacking the seagulls, killing their babies, and smashing their eggs out of the blue like this is nothing if not the worst form of brutality there is."

"Yes! Yes! That's right!" we began to shout, when the seagulls suddenly appeared overhead like bats out of hell and began diving down on us, tearing at us with their beaks. We tried to run away, our hands raised above our heads for protection, obscuring our view. Gunfire rang out, the sound of seagull cries indecipherable from human screams. We had no choice but to run to the President's house, as it was the nearest shelter available. His men had taken cover at the edge of one of the windows, volleying a steady stream of gunfire at the seagulls, a few of them falling to the ground.

In the midst of arguing with the President, we hadn't noticed that some of the fog had lifted, making for improved visibility. To boot, we'd made ourselves even more of a target by coming together in a single, shouting mass.

The argument abruptly came to a halt, cut short by everyone's immediate need for protection. The first thing we had to do now was to get out of harm's way. Arguing about whose fault it was would have to come later.

"Any bright ideas, anyone?" the President asked.

A state of temporary cease-fire now in effect, the Writer, who had taken on the role of being our collective spokesman, said, "There isn't much we can do. Let's go back home once night falls, making sure we don't attract too much attention, and wait for them to cool down. They can't keep up their attack on us forever."

The President evidently thought differently: he argued that it was necessary to respond to violence with even greater violence and was of the opinion that "there is to be no giving in to terror." Violence was to be used to intimidate, frustrate, and destroy the enemy. This was the only option, or else things would only get worse. It was out of the question for this attack to go unpunished. No matter how vehemently we pleaded and argued with him, it was totally in vain. He remained hell-bent on bloodthirst.

He looked us over with an air of authority and told us it was absolutely imperative to show decisiveness in these kinds of cases. We could not fall weak before the enemy. If we wanted to be secure within our homes, we had to be willing to take on the risk posed by this war.

"Have you forgotten, gentlemen, that I was the commander in chief of this country for years?" he then asked. "It's only natural that I would know how to deal with these types of matters better than you, so it's best you leave it to me."

To which Lara said, "It's for that very reason that things have reached this point—*you* were the commander in chief!" But the President, barely acknowledging her, began to speak of his war plans.

The frontline combat unit—which was to say, his men—would build a shelter overlooking the cove during the night. Though it would be a simple structure, it would be sufficient to keep the firing squads from getting hit. Taking up inside the shelter at night, the firing squads would open fire at dawn and wipe out the seagulls. The ammunition necessary for the job would be transported to the shelter at night.

We tried to tell from the expression on his face if he was actually serious, but then sadly realized he couldn't have been more serious. His lips were pursed; his fierce eyes, set with determination.

I wondered for the umpteenth time: Why is this man so evil? For many years I've had a habit of comparing people to animals. I think each one of us looks like some particular animal. Some of us have a face like that of a bird, and some like that of a sheep. Some of us look like a horse, with a long face just as a horse has, while others have the face of a wolf. It's my belief that we take on the personalities of the animals we resemble. I don't know, maybe it's just that it feels right to act like that animal. It's what comes naturally. So can you imagine asking a sheep, say, why it acts so tame? Or asking a wolf why its behavior is so predatory?

It was then that I realized what animal the President looked like. His thin, pursed lips were like a slit at the bottom of his face, their corners drawn downward. With his protruding cheekbones and the blank stare in his eyes, it was a shark he resembled—and to a tee. I was surprised that I hadn't noticed this before, and thought, "So. This is his nature, then—the nature of a shark." Asking him why he was so cruel would have been as absurd as asking a shark why its teeth were so sharp. This was how he perceived the world. I wanted to share this thought with Lara and the Writer as soon as possible, adding my two cents to our previous discussion. But now was neither the time nor the place to do so.

As night fell, we left the shark to his war games and went home.

The seagull lay stiff in the living room. I didn't know what I was going to do with it. What did one do with a dead seagull? Bury it? Toss it in the trash? I took it in my hand. "Ugh! What on earth are you doing!" Lara asked. "I'm examining the dead seagull," I said.

Inspecting it up close, I saw that its beak was broken, a piece of it barely hanging from a stringy tendon. It looked so pitiful, I thought, with its broken neck, its broken beak. What it had died for had hardly been worth it. There was no more than a broken window to show for its self-inflicted death. And though glass was hard to come by on the island, it could be shipped in, and the window restored.

What they had actually achieved, paying for it with a grisly death, was to frighten everyone, instilling terror in people's hearts. And the truth was that for this alone, suicide simply wasn't worth it. Fear, too, after all, was a temporary emotion. It was possible for a person to be afraid one day and forget all about it the next, getting lost in the details of daily life and going on to laugh again.

As I stared at the seagull in my hand, something occurred to me: that the suicide-bomber seagulls had been designated from among those who had lost their young. They might have even volunteered themselves. It would have been one way to escape the hideous pain of having lost their children.

At any rate, a dead seagull wasn't exactly a pleasant sight to behold. Or at least that's the way I saw it, now that I perceived the seagulls with new eyes. Seagulls don't strike one as particularly warm creatures when they're alive, either, in any case. They have a cold and distant air about them; they don't cozy up to people, and they don't eat out of your hand. So that is why people have written folk songs in ode to nightingales, canaries, cranes, imaginary birds like phoenixes, and even crows and storks, and have never written even one ode to seagulls. Furthermore, there's never been an ode sung to a single seagull in particular, because whatever songs were sung were in praise of the sight of flocks of them along the shore. Still, this dearth of musical inspiration provided on the part of seagulls could hardly have created a reason for killing them and destroying their babies. The fact is that despite their cold and heartless appearance, the way they sacrificed themselves was undeniably moving.

The next day we stayed in again. There was no seagull attack this time, and calm apparently settled over the island, but we thought it best not to take any chances. It turned out to be a wise thing for us to have done, because that evening, disaster struck again.

Lulled by the quiet of the moment, our guitarist friend at Number 4 had gone wandering in the hills, only to fall prey to an attack by the seagulls, during which he fell off the cliff. They found him with a broken leg, a broken arm, and a massive gash on his temple. He lay in bed with a fever for days. Worst of all was that it would be a long time before he could play the guitar again. This small tragedy brought a lot of sadness to the islanders. Now some of us had begun to think that the seagulls had gone too far.

People were rarely going outside, only doing so if they absolutely had to, and even then, they would bring along a large pot or saucepan to hold over their heads, just in case. Our older and less agile friends weren't taking any chances, walking around with pots on their heads for fear of falling victim to another sudden strike, even enduring the discomfort of walking around with their heads bent back, peeking out from beneath the pots as they walked.

At night we would hear the clatter of the construction that was taking place. A day or two later, there was an announcement of the President/Shark's war plans. Using tree branches and a few large pieces of wood stripped from closets and wooden doors, his men had erected a blockhouse in a secure location overlooking the seagulls' cove. This giant closet was made in such a way that ten people could fit inside it, and place themselves in positions of safety via the long and narrow window that ran along its front wall.

After the President's men and a few of the islanders had finished building the blockhouse, once again they wasted no time in emptying out their guns on the seagulls. One morning a sharp ring of furious gunfire broke out on the island. Obviously enough, having begun the war at daybreak, they had surreptitiously taken cover in the blockhouse overnight. Once again the seagulls began to fall blood-soaked into the sea. We found out later on that this time there had been some islanders who had willingly shot at the birds, showing off their marksmanship as they did so. Like the others, this massacre also lasted till evening. As night fell, everyone went home.

There was little left for us to do, now that things had reached this point and an all-out war had broken out. We would sit in despair at home, making every effort to convince our neighbors not to go on with the war against the seagulls, discovering that the islanders, too, had begun to hate the seagulls.

The next day, surprisingly enough, nothing happened. We were anxiously awaiting another seagull attack toward morning, and were left standing by the window when it didn't materialize. Nothing was happening. With its lush trees, its houses buried among multitudinous shades of green, and its verdant coves, the island may well have struck a newcomer as a paradise on earth, a harbor of peace and tranquility—as it used to be.

The next day passed just as uneventfully, as did the day after that and the next few days that followed. Maybe the President/Shark's methods had been successful, scaring off the seagulls. The theory that violence could only be prevented with greater violence had begun to draw more and more adherents. Little by little in the meantime, folks had started to go outside again, getting caught up in the sweet nuisances of the routines of daily life.

From time to time, we'd shoot a glance across the distance at the seagulls' cove and see them standing watch over their eggs, some of them diving into the sea in their hunt for food. The war must have come to an end.

We took advantage of this period of stillness and made the necessary repairs to our home by ordering new windowpanes with a letter dispatched by the ferry. We began sipping wine among scents of cherry laurels, rose geraniums, and jasmine in the evenings again. And we made frequent visits to our guitarist friend, sharing cheerful anecdotes with him in our best attempts to chase away his blues. We didn't see so much as a glimpse of the President and his men.

And thus the days went on, all in a state of calm. But that was before the island got its first martyr.

We had a quiet, withdrawn friend who lived by himself at Number 14. He wasn't one to spend much time with the rest of us, setting off on his rowboat to go fishing early each morning and gathering the fishing nets he'd set out the night before. The friendship of the cigarettes that never left his lips was all the friendship he needed, it seemed. He was about fifty but looked even older, and was a man loved and respected by all. Exceptionally skilled in carpentry, he was always happy to lend us a hand with repairs we couldn't manage on our own. Rumor had it that he'd once owned a carpentry studio, and that he'd settled on the island after losing his wife in a fire that had broken out in it.

It was this friend of ours who was the victim of an attack by the seagulls shortly after taking off for the open sea on his boat early one morning. Though I didn't witness it myself, according to those who looked on in terror from the shore, hundreds of seagulls descended in a throng on the defenseless man. They began to peck at him, shrieking with a frenzy as they ripped into him with their beaks. The blood gushing from the poor man's head could be seen even from shore. A few people ran home for their guns so they could shoot the seagulls, but as he tried to stand up inside the boat, trying at the same time to protect his head between his hands, the poor man lost his balance and fell into the water. Yet the seagulls were relentless; when the man rushed up for air, they tore his flesh to pieces. A halo of blood began to form around the man's head. He would grasp at the air with his hands, sinking and resurfacing, sinking and resurfacing, over and over again, so that even his hands were red.

And that was how we lost our dear neighbor the carpenter. They brought his body back to shore an hour or two later, after pulling it out of the water before the currents had dragged it out to sea. We were struck with grief. It was only now, you might say, that we were beginning to realize just how savage the seagulls could be. We were filled with hatred by the things they had done—to an innocent person! Although it was unlikely we'd have felt such sorrow if their victim had been the President or his men, this had turned into a bloody tragedy in which the ones to lose their lives were not those who had set the war in motion.

We buried the carpenter the following day at nightfall, next to our neighbors who had died of natural causes and who had expressed their wish not to be transferred to the mainland after their death. Some of our neighbors had been so traumatized by this onslaught that they came to the funeral holding stewpots over their heads and guns in their hands.

The lurid fate of the eccentric carpenter left us all in tears. The neighbors were whispering, "Damn those seagulls! What could they have wanted with that poor man?" The President and his men didn't say a word throughout the ceremony, silently watching events take their course. Grief-stricken, we said nothing, because we simply couldn't think of what to say. We were well aware of both the depth of our mourning and the lethal hatred of the seagulls that had come over all of us. The circumstances being what they were, no one would have dared to say, "But we were the ones who attacked the seagulls in the first place, and now they've struck back. We're the ones who are guilty here!" All logical arguments about any of this had lost all meaning. Everyone wanted revenge. Fear fed hatred, and hatred fed fear. I was stupefied, quite unable to talk. When I got home, I found Lara crying softly at the fate of the carpenter whom she'd loved so much. She said: "The President is the murderer!"

"Best you don't go saying that to anyone, whatever you do," I said. "No one's going to listen to such common sense when so much rage has gripped everyone. Hold your tongue. Please, for my sake."

I knew that the seagulls were now the islanders' greatest enemy. Everyone was trying to come up with ways to get rid of them. Yet finding one was far from easy. The seagulls had not been intimidated, had not given up in the face of violence, and had taken revenge at every opportunity. At this rate, every new attack would only provoke them further and make life on the island all the more unbearable.

Everyone felt a dreadful daily sense of desperation. Life had lost all its appeal for the islanders, who had acquired the habit of walking quickly while holding saucepans over their heads, gingerly lifting them up at their edges like helmets every now and then, tilting their heads back in fear as they looked out for the seagulls. They would gather at the shore, and, as the seagulls dove in and out of the sea, slicing the air like knives, the islanders would look on with hatred in their eyes. Plans of destroying them were discussed amid whispers at night. The plans ran the gamut, ranging from pouring gasoline on the seagulls' cove and burning it to asking for help from the military units.

As for me, quite frankly, I didn't know what to think. The Writer and Lara refused to blame the seagulls, never once letting themselves forget how matters first began. Though I didn't let on, I found myself unable to agree with them. After seeing the seagulls' savagery, it was as though something had broken inside of me. True, they didn't start the war, but this sure as hell was no way to live. If only none of this had ever happened!

What can I say, my dear Writer friend: I've never been able to be either as resolute or as determined as you. I haven't had the courage to be as independent in the way I think, nor to be on my own as much as you. As always, you were right, and so was Lara: sticking up for what was right was the best means of avoiding greater harm in the future, but now I can admit that the seagulls' brutality had frightened me, too. The way they had put our guitarist friend in bed, and their utter savagery in pecking our poor carpenter friend to death, hadn't left a single trace of sympathy for them within me. Maybe, in some romantic fashion, my tender, waffling heart preferred innocent victims to warriors out for revenge.

The islanders' hatred of the seagulls and their search for ways to do away with them had no doubt pleased the President enormously. It was exactly what he'd been after all along, having turned an enemy that had once been his alone into a common target of hatred.

He explained his thoughts on the matter at a secret meeting, as we could no longer meet openly, not wanting to attract attention. He said it was necessary to attempt a brand-new tactic in the fight against the seagulls. The first rule of war was to pit your enemy against other enemy forces.

After our neighbors finished applauding this apparent stroke of genius, the President/Shark explained his astounding war strategy: foxes were to be brought to the island. The foxes would decimate the seagull population by stealing the seagulls' eggs and eating them. The fact that there were no foxes on the island had been why the seagulls' numbers had grown "as large as a pack of bitches," as he put it. This was the only hope the islanders had, according to him. Moreover, by using their advantage of intelligence and allowing the two species to attack each other, the islanders would be able to destroy the enemy without putting themselves in harm's way.

The President's words were met with drawn-out applause and cries of "Bravo!" The islanders were breathing easy for the first time in a long time, now that they at least had something on which to pin their hopes where the future was concerned. The foxes that were on their way were viewed by everyone as saviors that would exact revenge for the poor carpenter's death.

Despite the Writer's vociferous protests—about "the ecological balance" or something to that effect—no one was listening to him anymore. He had come to be labeled by the islanders as a dangerous troublemaker. A few people looked him over with contempt, with others expressing the opinion that his warnings were nothing more than those of an "intellectual blowhard."

As the meeting drew to a close, the President said, smugly: "As for how we're going to get ahold of the foxes, leave that to me, my dear friends. Having anticipated that you would decide in favor of this measure, just as you've done, I've already placed an order by satellite phone for twenty foxes, ten of them male and ten female. The villagers I used to go hunting with are going to send them over by ferry straightaway. We're going to be free of this scourge very soon now. Thanks to your decisive attitudes, I have nothing but complete confidence in our ability to rid ourselves of this plague upon the island. I'm proud of the dedication you've all shown for its sake. Long live our island, down with the seagulls!"

The crowd was still applauding and shouting "Down with the seagulls!" as we quietly left the scene.

We were in the minority now, and though we weren't admitting it to each other, it was also true that we had become afraid of the community; or, in other words, afraid of our neighbors and our friends.

14

I'**LL NEVER FORGET** the day you shouted at our neighbor friends, "What are you, stark raving mad?" Even your thinning beard seemed to quiver with rage as you held your hands out to either side, looked into everyone's eyes, and cried out, "Have you gone mad? Have you gone completely insane?!"

The only other time I've ever seen you so enraged was when you were arguing with the President. I used to witness your occasional bouts of anger, but never—apart from your argument with the President—had I seen you explode the way you did then. The intensity of your anger took us all by surprise. You were never a cheerful fellow, a shadow of grief forever wandering about your face, and you would have your tense moments, so I was under the impression that you had a secret you didn't share with us, a wound you kept hidden somewhere down deep. Lara and I would even talk about it from time to time, asking each other what it could be that was such a source of heartache to our dear friend. But your anger this time was far different. That, I imagine, must have been the day you realized that we had lost our island forever, even as we had yet to discover what it meant to lose an island.

Your reaction to the islanders' lack of concern reminded me of the story of Jesus's retreat into the mountains. You know the one—that wonderful story the two of us had once talked about. Seeing the Prophet running toward the mountain, bystanders were said to have asked him, "Oh, Almighty Jesus! Is it a lion you're running away from?"

"No!" Jesus was said to have replied.

"Is it a tiger—or perhaps a dragon?"

"No," said Jesus again, then added, "I'm the Prophet. I'm not afraid of lions or tigers."

"Then why are you running?" they asked him.

"I'm running away from the idiots," Jesus supposedly said. "When it comes to them, I don't stand a chance."

Our friends remained silent in the face of your irate questions—besides, what could they have said? They were bewildered by the events of recent days, with some wearing pots on their heads, while others wore saucepans. Skittish and frightened, they anxiously searched the sky every now and then as they listened to you speak.

"Why don't you try using your heads a little, my friends!" you continued. "Were the seagulls *ever* our enemies? In all these years, was there ever the least instance of conflict between them and us? Did you ever have the slightest problem with them before this man came to our island?"

A few people slowly shook their heads "no."

And yet I knew, although they said nothing to your face, that many of them spoke behind your back. I would happen to hear people speak ill of you from time to time.

"Well, now, wouldn't you know it! The guy fancies himself the seagulls' lawyer!"

"Seagulls, friends? What planet is *he* on?"

"And he thinks he's fit to be a teacher to us?"

"As if our friend laid up in bed weren't our friend!"

"The poor carpenter is dead."

"The nerve of him, actually *defending* those hideous, savage creatures!"

"After all this injury, all this destruction..."

Though I tried to defend you, I knew that it was pointless to expect they would change their minds. Fear had done such a number on their heads that getting them to see things any other way was no better than a pipe dream, at this point. They'd all invested their hope in the foxes, their "saviors." The foxes would come, eat the seagulls' eggs, and thus do away with these brutal creatures at their very roots, or so the theory went. Then the seagulls would get what they deserved. Though large numbers of them still thrived after the islanders had killed so many, it would be a whole other ballgame once the foxes arrived. And then we'd see if the seagulls could wear out the foxes like they had the humans.

T HE ISLANDERS spent that week in a state of suspense as they waited for the ferry that would come bearing the foxes. The long-awaited day arrived at last, and the grand white ferry came into view on the horizon. Feeling bolder after the cessation of the seagulls' attack, we gathered at the pier. The President and his men stood at its edge, staring out at the motorboat as it brought in an assortment of supplies from the ferry.

It drew up to the pier and, one after the other, cardboard boxes, specially protective wooden containers containing glass goods, and packages of food were unloaded onto the dock. There wasn't a one among them that bore semblance to a fox cage. The President frowned, looking worried.

His men asked the men on the boat where the foxes were. The ferry crew then hoisted up a large cardboard box and laid it at the President's feet. He flashed an order with his eyes for the men to open the box and remove its contents. The frozen-faced men presented him with a row of fox furs. The box also contained a letter, addressed to the President. One of the men read it aloud: "Dear Mr. President, on receiving your order, our hunters took immediate action and caught twenty foxes. In order not to damage the furs, we killed them with poison, preparing these furs for you with the utmost care. As the people of the region, we hereby express our gratitude for your having remembered us after all these years and for allowing us the opportunity to carry out your order."

"Idiots!" barked the President, kicking the box. "Once they've been turned into furs, what difference does it make whether they're male or female? Were your heads too thick for you to figure that out, too?!"

Long suffering from days fraught with tension, we island folk actually laughed for the first time in quite a while, but that just incensed His Holiness all the more.

"Get me that jackass who calls himself the governor—and do it now!" he shouted, and stepped into the motorboat that had been moored for days at the pier. The gadgets on the boat that we'd taken to be radar equipment apparently included a satellite phone, as well.

A while later the President's bellowing voice sounded from within the boat: "I asked you to get me live foxes, not furs... How, how... Yes, obviously, but... do you think I would have asked for ten males and ten females in that case? Since when have furs come in male and female, you fool!"

His face had turned purple by the time he reached the pier a few minutes later. He shot us all a hostile glance before spitting out: "There's been a minor delay in our plans. The foxes will be here next week!" Then abruptly, he took off.

The next week passed without incident. The seagulls stood watch over their eggs on their own cove as usual, and carried on flying about, doing no one any harm. It was as though a cease-fire had been declared. In time, the islanders gave up carrying pots and pans over their heads. What's more, thanks to the painstaking care with which our doctor had treated him, our guitarist friend was recovering more quickly than we'd expected. Though he didn't take up his guitar, his flutist friend would visit him often and play for him.

It was around this time that something happened to draw my attention. It apparently was of such little significance that it could easily have slipped my notice altogether. You remember the grocer's son I mentioned a while back? The peculiar, hunchbacked boy was such a familiar figure to us that we hardly noticed his existence. But on this particular day, he'd caught my attention; he seemed to be hiding something inside his jacket, glancing furtively this way and that as he rushed on, apparently agitated.

The boy's behavior was so strange and unexpected that I wouldn't have believed it if someone had described it to me. I was in the pines, in a location above the boy where he couldn't see me. Unable to resist my curiosity, I quietly began to follow him. The youth disappeared behind the grocery shop; when he returned a few minutes later, he was no longer hiding anything, his arms swinging freely at his sides. After he was gone, I went to the back of the shop.

Before me was a large chicken coop. The grocer would sell us the chickens and eggs he raised in the coop, from time to time cooking chicken instead of fish at the garden café. I wondered what the boy could be hiding there. I stood looking carefully, but saw nothing out of the ordinary. The chickens were wandering around inside the cage, clucking and pecking at their grains of feed. After looking a little longer, however, I noticed what they were busying themselves with was not only their food. They'd gathered around a few eggs. The eggs were a different shape and size than your ordinary chicken egg—they appeared to be rounder and whiter. Then suddenly it hit me clear as a bell what the boy was up to. I remembered the way he had crouched down and then stood up on the day of the seagull massacre. At the time, I hadn't been able to make any sense out of his actions, but it was plain to me now that he had been trying to rescue the eggs, secretly carrying them to the chicken coop and placing them under the chickens.

How strange the human species is, I thought. What you can discover in people in whom you would least expect to find it. Were the seagulls' eggs being accepted among the chickens? I wondered. Were the chickens keeping them warm, incubating them as they sat on them? There wasn't a single chicken on top of the eggs I saw among the straw, but I also couldn't see what was beneath some of the sitting chickens. Naturally he would know the chickens better than I, considering that he was the only one who entered the cage and gathered the eggs. Maybe this covert rescue operation was in fact serving some good, who knows.

"Good for you, kiddo!" I thought. "Clever idea!"

I was itching to tell the Writer and Lara about my discovery.

At any rate, here I've gone and digressed yet again...So, yes; as expected, the next week, the big ferry delivered a cage to the island. On seeing the foxes, restlessly circling around one another inside the cage as it was being removed from the motorboat, the President and the island community were in a state of rapture. You'd have thought it was rescue angels rather than foxes that had arrived, because such spontaneous gleeful applause resulted.

Decked out in white, the President—his face more shark-like than ever today, and his eyes drawn even closer together—broke out into a victory speech. The reign of the seagulls on the island was about to end. The sophisticated strategy of pitting an enemy against an enemy would take care of the problem at its very source. The islanders would be able to breathe easily again and look to the future with a feeling of reassurance. Very soon now, every nook and cranny of the island territory would be secure, and our community would be free of the threat of terror.

The President's speech was interrupted by frequent applause. A ceremony then accompanied the opening of the cage door. The foxes first paused, awakening from their travel sedation, then slowly drew up to the door and tentatively peeked their heads in and out of the cage. Then, all at once, the ten male and ten female foxes rushed off toward the forest and disappeared. Another species had been added to the creatures living on the island.

As the foxes ran, swinging their fat, bushy tails behind them, the President continued smiling, thoroughly pleased with himself, while the community applauded the rescuing heroes.

After the ceremony, we quietly dispersed and returned to our homes. Now that the watch for an attack had ended, this meant the island's period of violence was over. Everything seemed to be buried in silence. By all appearances, nothing had changed, and daily life went on as it had in the past, people greeting each other and making small talk. But there had been an unmistakably palpable change in the atmosphere of the island. There was no longer any trace of the lightheartedness and camaraderie there once had been, nor of the friendships that had been free of calculation and wariness.

The difference was even more pronounced when it came to us; which is to say, very few people were honoring any ties of friendship with the Writer, me, and Lara—virtually ostracizing us by the way they acted in our company. Some evenings, we would hear of get-togethers taking place at our neighbors' houses, but we were never invited.

The Writer was waiting for a chance to take revenge on all of the islanders anyway, and had no wish to be in anyone's company. It was as though his loneliness, reclusiveness, and anger had reached critical mass.

Lara and I weren't taking it so hard in the long run, because we were able to take comfort in the protective harbor we were to each other. But the Writer had no such comfort.

The most significant event to add a touch of color to those otherwise uneventful days was the birth of two seagull chicks inside the chicken coop, which I'd been secretly visiting from time to time to see how things were coming along. So the boy had met with success. He'd saved the lives of two baby seagulls. How he'd been feeding these two knock-kneed creatures that opened their mouths wide with a ravenous hunger to consume everything was a secret I never found out.

We never saw the foxes again after that day. They must have found lairs for themselves in the forest. Whether they were eating the seagulls' eggs wasn't possible for us to see, either. No one was in the mood to go and see the seagulls' cove; and besides, the memories were still too painful.

15

THE FOLLOWING EIGHT MONTHS elapsed in an uneventful manner. Basically, they were boring and monotonous, much like a blank page in a book. After so much drama, this break was a blessing...

16

...UP UNTIL ONE AFTERNOON, when I awoke to a woman's scream that brought back memories of the island's days of terror.

We islanders love to stretch out for a little cat-nap in the afternoons. Not having particularly busy schedules, we don't think of the habit as being a waste of time. While some of us may stretch out on a divan or hammock in our gardens, others of us may take shelter in the serenity of our beds beneath a comforter.

In the midst of our usual afternoon languor, we heard the scream and jumped to our feet. We scram-bled off in the direction it had come from, noticing that people had begun to gather in front of the house at Number 22. When we got there, the doctor was drawing blood, with the aid of a small pump, from the leg of the elderly woman who lived there.

A snake had bitten the woman as she was getting into bed for her afternoon nap. It had sprung out at her from within one of her bedcovers, which had been draped with a single fold over her bed.

A few of our neighbors had gone in search of the snake in the meantime. They finally cornered it in the bedroom closet and killed it. Dangling from the end of the stick that one of our brave neighbors held in his hand to show it to us, it was a creature so mottled and alien that it sent a cold fear shooting into our hearts. It somehow occurred to me that the brightness of the snake's colors meant that the snake was extremely poisonous. And I wasn't mistaken, as it soon turned out. Our friends with expertise in these matters explained that the snake was indeed a highly poisonous and dangerous breed.

Being unfamiliar with such cases, we were shaken by this news, being used to sleeping like babies with our doors unlocked and our windows open. We had never known any other danger since the seagull attacks, the bitter memories of which had begun to fade as time passed.

We simply didn't come across dangerous species of animals or poisonous plants to put our easygoing lifestyles at risk here. Or rather, that's how we'd seen it up until that day. Seeing the snake swinging from the end of the stick that our neighbor had held in his hand, and the heart-wrenching state of the poor woman trying feverishly to rid her body of the effects of the poison, was shattering the sense of security we'd been living with. Now we would have to look beneath our covers before getting into bed, inspect the steamy ceilings of our bathrooms after taking baths, peer inside our closets, and, in short, take all kinds of unnecessary measures for the sake of living with a sense of security.

But the thing was, where had this poisonous creature come from? How had it sneaked into the house? With our minds bothered by these questions, that night we slept fitfully and fearfully. We sensed an ominous course of events to come. We were not proven wrong.

Waking up to the chilly morning air as Lara still slept, I stepped out onto the terrace and, looking off to the right as I stretched my sleep-stiffened body, I saw it. There before me was a red and green piebald snake, its upper half erect as it hissed at me, threatening me with each lick of its forked tongue.

It was virtually identical to the one we'd seen the day before. Whether the fact that I froze in my spot proved the truth of legends concerning snakes or had more to do with feeling a shiver in my heart, I can't say. I can't remember ever having turned so limp and helpless as I had at that moment.

The snake was swinging back and forth and making angry motions; I took this to be a sign it was preparing to attack. I wanted to run away as fast as I could, and yet it was as though we had some secret pact between us, standing face-to-face like this. My sense that if I moved it would move too made it impossible for me to act.

And then a miracle happened. The snake was suddenly attacked and, with a blow to the center of its body, crushed. In the same instant, I saw Lara standing next to me in a shimmering white night-gown, a large garden shovel in her grip—the one she'd just used to deliver the fatal blow to the snake. I remember a dizzying mix of joy, relief, shock, and fear rising up in my throat in that moment. I hear my mind declare "How incredible! Lara just saved my life! She *saved my life!*"

Was this woman who had just delivered killer blows to the snake—not stopping at crushing it with the face of the shovel, but actually going on to behead it with the blade—the same sweetheart I'd always known? My waif-like Lara who was afraid of life? I perceived the intensity of her anger at that incredible moment as a measure of her love for me. It made me deeply gratified to see, with every blow she delivered to the snake, how much she feared for my life, and what a fight she would put up against any danger that threatened to take her lover away from her.

After I pried the shovel out of her hands, she eventually grew calm again, as if waking up from a violent dream, and as suddenly as a tropical rainstorm, she broke out in tears, her shoulders shaking. We put our arms around each other and went inside the house, but the house no longer felt safe. Nor did the garden. Danger, it seemed, lurked everywhere, and could jump out at us at any moment. Each and every dark and hidden corner—beneath the bed, inside the closets, the towel hanging in the bathroom, beneath the bushes, among the cherry laurels, or the trellis—could have been an ambush in which a poisonous enemy might have settled, lying in wait for us.

We made ourselves some coffee to pull ourselves together, sipping it without saying a word. Later, I gathered up the remains of the snake with the same shovel and threw them in the trash. Still feeling strangely shaken, I was unable to look at the crushed snake, but it was hardly something I would have requested Lara to do after all that she'd already done.

She was sitting in the seat in the garden, looking off into the distance as she cradled her legs, which she'd drawn up around her chest. Her face was ashen. I realized then that we hadn't spoken to each other that morning, not so much as a word.

Just then, I heard the screams I'd been expecting, and with a sense of doom on the horizon. Screams and commotion rose up from the island— the screams and commotion that had grown all too frequent for us within a mere matter of a day. Someone had undoubtedly been bitten by a snake again, as snake-killing ceremonies such as ours were lately becoming more and more common at some of the houses. Lara looked at me with anxious eyes and asked, "What are we going to do?"

"I don't know!" I said. Snakes had taken over our island, and we were all but at a loss as to what to do about it.

Late that afternoon, in a state of delirium, the elderly woman at Number 22 died in the arms of the helpless doctor. We buried her the next day next to our beloved carpenter as the islanders looked on, their faces having turned deathly pale with fear. The woman's husband cried an endless stream of tears, unable to believe what had happened.

The houses were teeming with snakes, and the doctor's supply of serum and medication was simply inadequate. We could see no other choice but to wait for the ferry. Some had begun to speak of leaving this island behind, feeling that the place had become cursed. We were consumed with rage, though we had no clear target to pin the blame on.

Although they had killed two snakes that had tried to enter the President's house, his men remained uneasy, and stood guard around the clock. It was only the President and his wife in the house now, because his grandchildren had left the island with a farewell ceremony before being sent off on the ferry in time for the start of the new school year. We didn't hear much from the President after that day. Even after all this precaution, exactly one week to the day after the first snake attack, the President, too, fell victim to a snake that bit him on the hand.

As people told it, he had been gardening when it happened and was preparing to prune his shrubs. His men, who immediately rushed to his side upon hearing him scream, managed to save him with an assortment of pumps, medications, and serums they whisked in off the boat. Though he lay in bed with fever and pain for days, he had escaped the life-or-death point of danger. This development had clearly shown that those on the boat were well prepared, as well as the fact that they weren't using their supplies for the benefit of the islanders. Even so, some of the islanders continued to defend him, turning a deaf ear to the opposition we'd managed to organize through the occasion.

What a strange island we'd become. The meetings the President had held in the early days of his presence on the island, the pruning of our trees, the beatings of the grocer's poor son, the insults we were subjected to, and the attacks on the seagulls had all been forgotten. As most remembered it now, everything had begun when those despicable seagulls had attacked us. It was as though a force from above had come and, as everyone slept, erased the memories of the island community overnight. On the few occasions when the three of us would have arguments with our neighbors, just as they would disagree with us whenever the subject arose—though they usually went easy on Lara and me—they would say peculiar things that seemed to place blame on the Writer. As they saw it, the frequently mentioned "he," with his talk of gloom and doom, was the one who had caused these disasters.

The fact was that the Writer had never had warm relations or any kind of close friendship with the islanders to begin with; he was, as they say, "in a league by himself," and withdrawn. Obviously, though, he had a secret that saddened him and made him distant from other people; apparently there was some shadow of suspicion hanging over his life, which you could also tell occasionally from the expression on his face.

So, my dear friend: this is how they spoke of you. Lara and I would defend you with all we had, protest that you were the most honest and most up-standing person we had ever known in our lives, but it was of no use. Nor am I saying these things merely for the sake of politeness. You really were the most honest and upstanding person we had ever known. I'll never forget all that I've learned from you, what you taught me not only through your words, but also through your actions, your courage, and at times, your firmness of purpose, which was perceived by everyone else as arro-gance. I suppose that if I'm to be completely truth-ful here, I should conclude many of my sentences with "Even if I don't always apply what I've learned from you." That's because I know that you wouldn't at all approve of what I call a literary trick, featured as Chapter 15. I know you're going to think that I've damaged the integrity of the story, even in the midst of the stirring narrative about the snakes' raid on the island, and that you'll probably even get mad, shooting darts at me with your eyes.

I know, believe me, I know, but I hope you'll allow me to have played around with the style just a bit here. Because I mean, a writer gets kind of bored after all, wouldn't you say? Narrate, narrate, narrate...always the same old sentences, the same old depictions, the same old images, the same old allegories, the same old metaphors. Events told in similar ways for centuries. What harm could there be in a little experimentation?

I can just hear you saying, "Hey you! Instead of trying to describe the monotony of life on the island with a blank page, why don't you say more about the foxes that came to the island in the previous chapter, you idiot!" And you'd be right; there's certainly more to be said on that count.

I HAD SAID that after the ten male and ten female foxes scampered off into the forest like a bolt of lightning, swinging their big, fluffy tails behind them, no one saw them again, right? According to experts in these matters and the information found in our encyclopedias at home, these foxes don't behave in a collective and organized manner the way seagulls do, but live solitary lives that revolve around hunting. They're said to have sly personalities, making use of every opportunity that arises before them, and eat up to a kilogram of food a day. This food consists of small animals, chickens, eggs, and even blackberries and strawberries. And, by the way, they frequently produce a lot of offspring.

We haven't been witnesses to their seagull egg–hunting skills, for which they were brought to the island, because we never saw them do that. The case would appear to be that they secretly steal those eggs and, without the awareness of the mother and father seagulls, make off with them and eat them. There were even those who asserted that the foxes had made significant headway in reducing the seagulls' numbers.

The foxes had come under much discussion around that time. Summoned by the President with an announcement distributed to each house, a few islanders touched upon the subject at another meeting that was held one evening at the café.

And a good thing, too, because it turned out to be a wake-up call. The island community once again stood planted around the tables that had been placed together to form a square around the room, and the members of the executive committee each took their place.

One of the seats reserved for them was empty, however. The Writer hadn't come to the meeting. Lately, he was never out and about, and he was neglecting Lara and me even though he knew it upset us.

Our musician friends were sitting in a corner of the garden, occasionally making sounds with their instruments and looking around as if they were in unfamiliar surroundings.

I was happy to see that our guitarist friend had recovered as much as he had. The President must have approached the musicians before the meeting and asked them to play something. Whatever it was, it sounded alien to me, unlike anything else they'd ever played before. On listening a little more carefully, I was able to make out that it was some kind of anthem.

The President, dressed in his immaculate white clothes, seated himself exactly in the middle with his usual authoritarian air. The only difference in his appearance since his arrival on the island months before was the gauze wrapped around his right hand. The musicians put down their instruments, and the meeting got under way.

As the discussions proceeded, I recalled our first meeting there. The one where the executive committee was elected and all those bureaucratic rules were established. And another meeting where the President tried to convince the islanders to launch an attack on the seagulls. Everything looked the same on the surface, but how different it was: there was no longer the same trust, nor the same cheerfulness there used to be among the islanders. A shadow of sorrow had settled over everyone's face. Neighbors were eyeing each other with suspicion. A heavy sadness and sense of doubt wandered throughout the atmosphere. The mood only grew all the more somber when the President invited everyone to stand for a minute of silence in memoriam of our beloved carpenter and the dear elderly lady who had died of snakebite. The seats at which these friends of ours once used to sit were left empty, their portraits placed on the table. Some shed tears in the midst of the silence.

A few seagulls were flying about over the sea at that moment, and the islanders eyed them with hatred. The President made one of his usual epic speeches, made reference to "the enemies" and condemned the seagulls again, and tried to explain away the snakes as a result of a lack of civilized living on the island.

As he saw it, the struggle waged against the seagulls had been a success, and now the struggle waged against the snakes would be won with the same resoluteness and determination. No one could make the islanders give up, was his summation of our communal resoluteness. "While a subversive or two who aimed to undermine the community's morale and high spirits had come out of the woodwork," he opined, "they had been unable to realize their traitorous ambitions and unable to upset the unity and common purpose of the island's people." Here, he meant the Writer and us. One or two people shot us nasty looks.

The President had taken the necessary emergency measures in the struggle waged against the snakes as well, having placed an order via satellite telephone for enough snake poison for every house on the island. This toxin would be shipped in by ferry in two days, distributed to all the houses. The President's words were met with applause. For the first time, a ray of hope glimmered in the eyes of most of us; let's face it, most folks were constantly looking suspiciously beneath tables, clad in boots and gloves and with clubs in hand, on alert for another snake attack. They looked at the President with eyes full of gratitude. All they had to do was hang in there for just a couple more days, and the President would save them from this red and green plague upon the island, too, or so they thought.

But just as they were letting themselves ease into the happy comfort of this news, a voice erupted from the back of the room, annoying them: "Aren't you going to explain why snakes have taken over the island, Mr. President?"

It was the Writer! He was skin and bones from all the weight he'd lost, his eyes sunken into their sockets. Standing there like a fugitive ascetic, he flooded the President with a barrage of questions before directing another stream at the islanders.

Why had snakes invaded the island? Where had they come from after years of no sign of them? What could explain the way the snakes had managed to enter every house and multiply a hundredfold? What law of nature had caused this to happen? How on earth was it possible for this important matter to go undiscussed? Could it be that Mr. President—who was now squirming with obvious discomfort in his seat—had something to hide?

The salvo of questions that rained like bullets on the meeting ended with the Writer's final question:

"Would *you* prefer to clarify the situation, or shall *I*?"

As the President muttered something to the effect that there was nothing to be said, his men stepped toward the Writer, but he said that he was still a member of the executive committee and that he therefore had the right to speak. The men, their eyes hidden behind dark glasses, stopped with a motion of the President's hand.

Then, walking toward the very middle of the conference tables, the Writer spoke:

"Look here, friends. Remember how it all began. Think back to the days of the past, that happy time on the island when we got along with the seagulls, just as we got along with all of the living creatures on the island. You must have forgotten about all that. You know, back when we would watch the seagulls soar through the sky, when we would carry on conversations with each other in peace, and when we would listen to the sounds our musician friends would create with their flutes and guitars in such a way that those sounds were like part of the very nature that surrounded us. Those days when we would walk without fear beneath the shade trees…"

After searching the expressionless faces of the islanders as they listened to him, he continued:

"Don't you remember any of this? Before the arrival of this man, the pruning of our trees, the rules, the government, the notices distributed to our houses, and finally, the attack launched on the innocent seagulls."

At this point, an objection arose from Number 1, who by now had become one of the President's most loyal followers: "What does any of this have to do with the snakes?"

The Writer looked at him with calm composure and said, "It's got plenty to do with it, my old friend, plenty indeed." Turning toward the others, he continued:

"You brought foxes to the island to reduce the seagulls' numbers. Your enemy's enemy, supposedly, was your friend. According to the President's theories, you had no choice but to pit one enemy force against another. While the foxes quickly reduced the seagull population by eating their eggs, their own numbers multiplied. And as their numbers multiplied, not only did the seagull population shrink, but it also turns out we got more snakes."

"So what?" shouted a few neighbors as they shot another round of nasty looks.

"Friends—don't you get it? The snakes have increased because you've upset nature's balance. Because in the past, the seagulls would hunt the snakes. As a result, the number of snakes on the island never grew beyond a certain limit. And we certainly never ran into any of the poisonous kind, meaning that they were living far away from us, keeping to themselves. When the foxes reduced the number of seagulls on the island, the snakes' numbers grew and began to creep as far as into your houses. Which is to say, the foxes you've pitted against your enemy have become an entirely new threat that you failed to anticipate."

Silence hung in the air. I could almost hear everyone thinking "Could he be right?"

WHAT YOU SAID had made sense, after all. In fact, even the notary gentleman stood up to say, "Our friend is right. Tinkering with nature's balance always leads to disaster!" After that respected opinion was voiced, everyone seemed to have grasped the sad truth.

Nor can I deny our surprise when we saw that the President, for his part, was not in the least taken aback by your words, even assenting with a nod of his head. How was it that the Shark could have paid any attention to words containing such reason? I would have thought that after your speech, he'd have stood up and hurled insults at you, called upon the islanders not to listen to you and given orders to his men to arrest you or something like that. But no, apparently his political maneuvering over the years had taught him to retreat on some points and hide his evil intentions behind a mask of complete innocence.

THE PRESIDENT stood up, then said, "We have no choice but to accept that our friend here is right. I believe in being fair. A spade is a spade. The struggle we waged against the seagulls was a necessary one. Our paradise of an island could not have been handed over to those savage, pestilent creatures; besides which, we've always made these decisions by means of a vote and in a democratic manner. Isn't that right, friends? Everything has been done in a way consistent with the principles of democracy, and the attack on the seagulls was carried out on the basis of a majority decision. But what are you going to do? Unanticipated results like this can ensue from any struggle. One assesses the situation and takes measures accordingly. What matters is that we remain firm, remain united, maintain our morale."

In a tone more sarcastic than before, the Writer then said, "So then, Mr. President. What do you suggest we do now? Will we be starting a war against the foxes for the sake of giving the seagull population a little boost? Are we going to take up arms and go fox hunting?"

Assuming the most iron-willed expression he could, the President replied, "No! A thousand times no! We have no right whatsoever to go increasing the seagull population all over again, just when we're this close to a victory. They are the enemies of this island and everyone on it." He raised his voice so that it boomed before he continued: "We have yet to forget how they killed the poor carpenter in their thirst for blood, how they pecked to the death at our innocent neighbor's head. Have we forgotten, friends? Tell me, have we?"

"No, we haven't!" came a few shouts from the crowd.

Lowering his voice, the President went on: "But, my dear neighbors, we aren't going to sit on our hands and do nothing because things are the way they are; there's much to be done. For starters, let's wait for that ferry bearing the poison and rescue our houses from the threat of the snakes."

My gaze drifted toward the horizon for a moment as the discussions droned on. The sun was once again setting into the sea like a crimson disk, reflecting red, violet, and a thousand and one eloquent colors in between on the horizon. The seagulls were soaring through the sky with an ease reminiscent of a calm and peaceful holiday island. The island was, it seemed, just as it used to be, as though nothing had changed; we were the ones who had changed.

Lara did not break the silence she'd buried herself in on the heels of the incident with the snake, including at that meeting, as her distress was too great. After we got home, the only thing I knew to do was to respect her silence. Obviously enough, she was grappling with questions too heavy for words. As she slept in the night, she would emit little screams, twisting and turning.

How obvious it was that her distress had to do with her having killed that snake. I had seen with my own eyes how someone so thoroughly opposed to violence could turn into a killing machine when forced to that point. The sight of her breaking the snake's spine, then smashing a part of its body, and finally driving the blade of the shovel all the way through its neck to cut off its head was a sight I couldn't put out of my mind. So, fear can make people do anything, I thought. That perplexing question in my head that was so concerned with good and evil had now grown even more convoluted. There were no simple answers.

I left her alone at home the next day and went out for a walk on the island, realizing that she needed some time to herself. The truth was that I also felt the need to be alone with my thoughts for a while, given the issues now in my mind after Lara's act of courage when I had merely stood there, paralyzed: Was I a coward? Was I a weak and passive man who didn't deserve to be with her? Why hadn't I spoken up and objected to the President at meetings, despite the Writer's urgent pleas? Distraught at these questions, I went to Purple Water in hopes of finding him there, but there was no sign of him. Then just by wandering, I found a spot beneath the giant pine-nut trees, taking shelter in their protection and serenity.

The grocer's son was sleeping peacefully at the base of one of the pines. Pine needles and pine cones snapped and crackled under my feet as I walked. I managed to sit beside him, making as little noise as possible. The boy had fallen into a deeply peaceful sleep, as though no threat of seagulls or snakes existed on the island. He was sleeping with his mouth open. Not one of us had bothered to concern ourselves with this youth who never spoke, never communicated with anyone, never made eye contact with anyone; nor had any of us tried to understand what kind of a person he was. It had been enough for us to know him simply as the grocer's mentally disabled boy. He was an odd one, who moved as though he were swimming through water and whom we would see when he made his rounds of the houses. That was why it had surprised me to realize that he was trying to save the seagull chicks, and what had led me to pay attention to him.

He must have felt my presence there, because after a while, he woke up. He shot up suddenly, rubbed his eyes, and assumed an apologetic expression.

"You were sleeping so soundly," I said, "that I couldn't bring myself to wake you up."

Bewildered, unused to being spoken to, he tried to pull his eyes away.

"How are your guys?" I asked.

As usual, he remained silent, giving no reply. I could sense his fear.

"You know," I said, "the seagulls in the coop. Have you been able to save any other chicks besides those two?"

He took off running. As I watched this poor boy dash down the hill, I was filled with both compassion and a deep respect.

17

WORDS CAN DESCRIBE emotions and thoughts, and even images and actions, but I know of none that could even begin to describe the abominable smell of that snake poison that arrived on the boat and was subsequently placed among the gardens of each house, beneath the terraces, and at entrance and balcony doors. If there were a smell so bad it could break your nose, this would be the one. Suffice it to say, it would take piling up a hundred dead animals and letting them bake in the sun for days to produce anything close.

Delivered in barrels and liberally administered throughout the island, the poison may well have been chasing away the snakes, yet what misery we had to endure every time we entered our own homes! Not even the scent of those beautiful rose geraniums and jasmines was enough to cover up the offense. Though we sprinkled colognes throughout our homes and rubbed on lotions, and the women dug into their storage trunks to spray on their heaviest perfumes, none of it was of any use. "Ah, to hell with it! If the snakes come, so be it! It's better than dying of this smell!" some were even saying, washing away the poison surrounding their houses with soap and water, managing to alleviate the smell somewhat.

Poor islanders!

These poor people who'd walked around with pots and pans over their heads in fear of a seagull attack and donned their bulkiest boots in that sweltering heat because of their fear of the snakes now had to keep their noses pinned shut with clothespins. A few people had already begun to speak of the island as being doomed. Stricken with a curse. It made no difference how much we tried to argue otherwise; we were simply unable to convince them to the contrary, or that the island had been the most beautiful place in the world up until the President arrived. The island was cursed, and that's all there was to it. Who'd have known it—it was all a part of the island's fate! A few families had even begun to think about taking the ferry back to the mainland.

On noticing that the smell of the poison had grown lighter among the homes of those of our friends who'd washed it away, we set to doing the same as they had. Besides, the snakes surely had cleared off by now anyway, leaving us free to do something we hadn't been able to do in ages; that is, to take a breath of fresh air.

I'd been thinking that if I were a snake, I wouldn't want to go near any of these houses, but it turned out I was wrong: as soon as the effect of the poison began to wear off, snake sightings were reported by one or two of the houses. It was said that the snakes hadn't actually entered the houses, but had been caught in the garden or on the terraces. The snake-ousting project had thus apparently failed. Desperate, the people of the island appealed to the executive committee, which, of course, included the President.

With a determined face, the President responded by saying that everything would be taken care of, that an expert had been called in from the mainland to see to the snake scourge, and that this expert coming from across the sea would rescue us from all these troubles once and for all. This prominent expert had worked miracles elsewhere, ending problems and resolving crises, so there was no reason why he couldn't end our island's problems or resolve our island's crises. He finished his words with, "Our presidency considers and undertakes any measure necessary for security, welfare, and peace on the island. What matters is that you remain united, and that you be at ease."

Whipped up into a froth of excitement on hearing these words, the island's people looked to the horizon in anticipation of this talented expert. Then there was the matter of this expert's fee, which wasn't cheap. It would be necessary for each household to pay a certain amount as soon as the expert set foot on the island. Some among us suggested that we first see what he was going to do and pay him accordingly, but the other neighbors looked with derision at those who issued these warnings.

I kept quiet, because the things I'd experienced in recent months had taught me a life lesson that has stayed with me ever since: whatever you do, never attempt to rob the islanders of their dreams. Never tell your neighbors who wish to hang on to a certain hope that their hope is a pipe dream, and never urge them to be realistic. Why? Because people who are suffering hardship have a need to take refuge in some hope, even if it's a lie and leads them to hate those who tell the truth. And even if time should eventually prove you right, it doesn't matter, because by then they'll have forgotten the way things were in the beginning. Besides, how else could you explain the way the Writer had become the target of so much hatred, especially since he no longer mixed in with nor spoke to anyone in the community anymore!

I saw it best simply to shut up and pay my share of the fee, and to say nothing in reaction to this "expert" initiative. I didn't raise a single objection to those who gathered in little groups of threes and fives, praising the man for his talents and for having saved the country from numerous calamities, claiming that he was going to solve the problems on the island at their very roots. I merely suggested to Lara that we start thinking about what we would do if the expert's intervention were to turn into a fiasco, just as the other "initiatives" had. Perhaps it was also time for us to flee this island, but the thought of returning to the homeland filled us with dread. After leading a quiet and simple life for all these years, we would both have to find jobs and work. The matter of how we would adapt to the violence of the cities aside, how were we going to protect ourselves from Lara's ex-husband, who was bound to pick up her trail sooner or later?

Whenever we thought of these things, we would decide to stay on the island in spite of the snakes, only to conclude that life here, too, had grown unbearable, and so we spent our days wavering between the two.

One evening, we shared our fears with the Writer and asked him what he thought about the situation. With the circle of hatred that had come to gradually surround him, did he want to return to the homeland?

I 'LL NEVER FORGET the expression on your face at that moment, my dear friend. Your eyes were clouded with worry. After thinking long and hard about the answer to this question, you said, as if cracking open a treasure chest packed with secrets: "Going back is out of the question!"

You spoke with such alarm in your voice that Lara and I gathered at that point that your "inability" to return had to do with a serious matter indeed. And then you added: "If I were to return, they would never let me live."

I shuddered, as if what he said was a premonition of what was to come. There must have been so much worry written on my face as I looked at you at that moment, but turning it into a joke, you said, "Oh, come on, don't make such a big deal out of it. We're here for now, aren't we? We're living a life of security, arm in arm with the President's men and the snakes. Of course, which of the two is more dangerous, I couldn't say, but..."

It was more the bitterness in your voice rather than what you actually said that made such an impression on me.

IN RECENT DAYS, even the sea surrounding our island had begun to take on a frightening quality in my eyes. I shuddered at the sight of the tides that I used to take so much pleasure in watching as I sat on the shore, and at the times I'd play a game of picking out which of every seven waves was the biggest, having since come to sense both savagery and peril within the swell and fall of the sea. As the worry within me grew, it wasn't the sea's glistening surface I thought of, but the darkness within its depths. What could explain the evil of sharks and the goodness of dolphins when both lived in the same sea, under the same conditions? Then again, evil—but relative to what? Good—but relative to what? Maybe good and evil didn't exist as such.

"Ah," I said to Lara, "my dear, I'm utterly at a loss as to what to do anymore. I'm not as sure of things as I used to be. I can't trust myself any more than I can trust what I write. The only thing that gives me any sense of having any value in this life is being with you. Without that, I have no importance, I have no value."

With an invisible fabric woven with teardrops, pleasure, and tenderness, we would wrap each other. Those moments really were the most—maybe the only—valuable moments of my life.

The biggest thing missing from the Writer's life was that he didn't have a woman like Lara. I felt such pity for him because of it, and wondered: Had he never fallen in love? Was there no one he loved? Despite the closeness between us, I sensed that he wouldn't want to talk about this subject and said nothing about it.

Even saying what little he said that day must have been a major act of opening himself up to us. Life never ceased to surprise me in the meantime. On one of those days amid that troubled period, the grocer's son unexpectedly came and knocked on the door. He took my hand, pulled me outside, and began taking me somewhere. I was too surprised to say anything. I let the hunchbacked youth lead me where he wished, my hand in his, utterly in suspense and surprise. But when I saw that he was taking me in the direction of the chicken coop behind the grocery, I assumed he wanted to show me the seagulls.

And he did—but there was more. The boy opened the cage door and scooped up into his hands two seagull chicks that had grown strong, plump, and healthy. He carefully closed the cage door, and then we were off again. When we got to the edge of the pine forest overlooking the cliff, he gave me one of the seagulls. As if holding a baby, I tentatively placed my hands around the bird. It was warm, and I could feel the beating of its heart.

The boy then looked at me and released the young creature in his hands into the chasm. The baby bird struggled to fly, awkwardly flapping its wings, then alighted on a large jutting rock a few meters below.

The precipice we were standing at the edge of was high up, the waves visible down below as they hit the rocks and crashed in a burst of foam. I felt my feet slip on wet grass, fear rising up from my legs into my stomach. I stood back some. Meanwhile, the kid went on standing at the very edge of the cliff, watching the bird in amazement as it tried to fly. I had never seen such a look of happiness on his face before.

At the boy's signal, I, too, released the warm body in my hands. In the same awkward manner, it flapped its wings before alighting on a rock shelf. Then they both rose up into the sky, making an all-out effort as they flew a few meters farther. They rested for a moment and did it again.

The boy's face had lit up with the most luminous smile—the first I'd ever seen him smile at all. Out of the blue, he took my hand, seized by paroxysms of triumph. Just then, noticing the two fledglings, the other seagulls arrived on the scene and began to circle around them as if wanting to help them fly. It seemed to me that they were shrieking with delight. The sight of them pleased the boy even more, so much so that he began to laugh, his hand cupped over his mouth, staggering and striking strange poses in a show of his exultation.

The ceremony of releasing the birds to fly—or should I say, the fact that he had invited the one person who had known and kept his secret—made my heart ache. He was savoring the joy of giving those fledglings their lives, adding to his happiness by sharing it with me. His pure goodness overwhelmed me. But I promised myself not to think about all that.

The one note of sadness about that day on which I'd experienced this little moment of jubilation was seeing the dramatic fall in the numbers of the seagulls on their cove and the desolation that had settled over it. Laced with waning clusters of seagulls, the long shore that had once teemed with white birds now looked melancholy indeed. It was clear that as the steadily multiplying foxes stole the eggs, they were destined to wipe out the seagull population from the island.

18

WHAT A WELCOME it was—such pomp and circumstance! We did everything but scatter roses before the so-called expert, seeing as how he'd come to put an end to all our woes and deliver us from evil. Any successful professional who no doubt had received much praise over the course of his long life would have been bowled over by this reception.

When the boat dropped anchor in the bay, all except for the few islanders who were absent had taken their places along the pier. They squinted their eyes in an attempt to get a glimpse of this influential man, keeping watch in the meantime for a suitable moment to ask for help from those of their neighbors who had come better prepared with binoculars. They began a barrage of questions to those peering through them.

"Do you see him?"

"What sort of man is he, then?"

"What does he look like?"

I could hear one of my neighbors who was standing next to me, holding binoculars up to her eyes, replying to these excited questions. "Yeah, I see him. He's just come down off the ferry steps. He's getting on the motorboat now. He's taller than everyone else around him, and he's wearing a straw hat and sunglasses. He's a thin man, and tall—*very* tall."

"You're kidding me, man! Lemme see!"

No other visitor to the island had ever aroused so much excitement—not even the President. No doubt this commotion was caused by all the stories the islanders had told one another over the course of the week as they waited impatiently for their savior to arrive. Tales like: the expert had once rescued an agricultural area from a grasshopper raid without having to burn a single wheat crop; on another occasion, he had saved a fearful town from an imminent flood by miraculously changing the course of a riverbed. There were a few who went so far as to say that this expert had developed a special language for communicating with animals, and that he even had, incredibly, the power to trap lightning bolts with his bare hands.

Considering the infrequent communication the island had with the rest of the world, it was a mystery how everyone was getting wind of such news of his improbable feats. Whether or not they knew any of them were true, they nevertheless spoke with the utmost certainty.

Needless to say, the Writer wasn't there. We knew his deep disgust with these kinds of things and that he had opted to retreat into a life of solitude. But the interesting thing was that the President had also failed to show up at this reception. It must have been to preserve his position of authority—envying, perhaps, all the interest the islanders were showing in the expert. And perhaps he was taking the imperious approach that a newcomer's duty was to pay a visit to the President as his first act.

The motorboat drew near, and, true to the description given by our neighbors peering through binoculars, the silhouette of a very tall man emerged into view. It was almost as though Don Quixote was approaching us, albeit not on his horse, but on a motorboat. Just as the boat was about to make contact with the pier, everyone broke into applause. The expert received this outpouring of love with a nod of greeting and a mild-mannered smile, then jumped nimbly up onto the pier and shook hands with the crowd. Our neighbors were virtually swooning with delight. They were overjoyed, as though the man's height—which, I'm guessing, was at least six foot five and allowed him to look down on us—were advance evidence of the miracles he would work on the island. Behold! Our savior had come at last—and would put an end to our troubles!

While everyone had wanted him to be a guest in their home, this honor was given to Number 9, probably because he had a small guest house in his yard.

We eagerly anticipated an impressive speech from the expert, but alas, he preferred to remain silent. As soon as the hand-shaking ceremony had come to a close, he went off with the President's men to pay the statesman a visit. His enigmatic silence caused the assumed legend to grow larger, bolstering opinions that he was truly a man of importance. Instead of talking about his own repute or influence, he offered only a vague smile. The effect of his presence made us feel as though he were granting us a privilege, bestowing a gift upon us.

The expert remained silent throughout the week he stayed on the island, except for a couple of points of instruction he considered to be of special importance; as a result, the respect he received among the island population grew all the more.

We couldn't know just what it was he discussed with the President, but a torrent of instructions followed that afternoon. The President's men seemed to have come under his orders. They told us they didn't have much time for us. We were informed that we would have to work long and hard all that week erecting pillars at various sites across the island. It was a job with a critical deadline, and wasting time would not be tolerated.

We hadn't the faintest idea how these pillars were to be erected or what they were to be used for, but this didn't stop anyone from working like mad the next morning. While we toiled, the highly paid world-renowned expert stood on the hilltop, pointing out the work to be done with his long fingers. He would occasionally mumble beneath his breath, saying nothing other than those few incomprehensible words.

The islanders set about furiously cutting down trees from the forest, and transporting the logs. This time it was the President's men who were their biggest helpers, displaying the same skill as when they'd first come to the island while they now went about working side by side with the islanders. I wondered whether anyone remembered the old arbor made up of intertwining branches that arched across the sky.

The question in my mind still remained: What end was to be served by all this feverish work, all the trees that had been cut down, the small platforms placed on top of them, and all the poles being set up with Herculean effort? What was the purpose of it all? Having long forgotten about the notion of work owing to their years of indolence, the islanders began to have a number of questions of a rather disgruntled nature, as beads of sweat rolled down their noses amid this backbreaking work they'd suddenly thrown themselves into. The mood spread like wildfire, with everyone starting to ask, "What is it we're working for? What's the point of it all?" As the expert watched the work being carried out, the most fearless among us went to him to ask these questions.

Pretending at first not to hear the questions—or ignoring them as if they weren't worth answering—the expert saw the crowd around the questioners grow to include all of the islanders. Noticing they had left their work behind, he deigned to open his mouth and muttered, "The storks!" Then he turned around and walked off. No one had the courage to stop him—which, in my opinion, was because everyone was basically intimidated by the man's height.

"What'd he say?" everyone asked each other.

"What'd he say?"

"I think he said, 'The storks.'"

"What's that supposed to mean?"

"The storks, the seagulls, the snakes, the foxes... what do you suppose they all have in common?"

Our neighbors, now engrossed in this little game, were doing their best to solve the riddle.

At long last, someone figured it out: "Storks hunt snakes!"

"So?"

"What do you mean, 'so'? With storks on the island, there won't be any more snakes."

"So is the expert going to bring storks to the island? How's he going to do that?"

"OK, so we get the storks, but then why have we been setting up all these poles?"

Lara interrupted at this point and said, "For the storks! Don't you get it? Don't storks build nests on poles? He's building nests for them."

"Hey, you're right, we didn't think of that! So how's he going to bring the storks here? By sending them invitations?"

"OK, I've figured it out," the notary said, bringing the conversation to a halt. "Haven't they been saying it's got to get done just in time, that we have to erect all the poles this week? Well—there's a reason for it. Don't storks migrate south at this time of year, each year?"

"Yeah, they do. And they fly over the island on their way."

"So there you go. It seems the expert is going to make it possible for them to land on our island by preparing nests for them."

We saw everyone's eyes light up. The quandary was solved at last. The storks would come to our island, hunt the snakes, and save us from this misfortune. I was inclined to doubt the storks would look down from the sky and descend on a bunch of nests that had been prepared for them, but when I'd had an objection in the past, I always preferred to keep my mouth shut. Besides, the expert must have known what he was doing, being the great expert that he was.

Now that they'd solved the mystery, the people of the island began to work with even greater enthusiasm than before and to get the nests ready for the storks. Made of vines, the nests were placed on the platforms on top of the tall pillars that had been erected, thus resulting in what may well have been the only stork hotel in the world. It sounded mad, but not necessarily if you stop and consider all the strange things there actually are in the world.

That evening, while we were discussing whether this business was possible or not, out of the blue, we got a visit from the Writer! We greeted him, full of excitement at seeing him, not knowing to what we owed this honor. Lara had missed him terribly; they got along great and saw eye to eye on many topics. Yet lately it had seemed to us as though the Writer had turned his back on us, neither coming to visit nor calling to check up on us. We were never able to reach him whenever we tried calling him. Anyway, the past was the past, and what mattered was that he was now with us here in our yard. His visit overwhelmed us with delight.

"Kids, I need your help."

"Sure," we said, "what can we do for you?"

"These idiots have now gone and put their hopes in that quack they call an expert. 'Poles are going to be built and storks are going to come land on them,' they say. And again, they're only going to be disappointed."

"I think so, too," said Lara. "That's the most ridiculous plan I've ever heard of! But everyone's believed in it so much that they're not about to listen to any warnings."

"Even so," said the Writer, "let's go ahead and warn them. If they don't listen, they don't listen. Time will prove soon enough who was right."

"They've hardly learned any lessons from any of the warnings or from any of the misfortunes they've experienced so far, though," I added. "Regardless, what can we do to help you?"

He had prepared an announcement, which he asked us to copy by hand and distribute to all the houses.

I doubted this plan would do much good, but, not wanting to hurt the Writer, I immediately took pen and paper in hand along with Lara, who began producing one beautifully handwritten flyer after another.

"Dear neighbors," the announcement began, going on in an attempt to remind its readers of old times on the island. Was there anyone among us who remembered those good old days, I wonder? Or had everyone thoroughly lost their memory? Of those days when people didn't interfere in each other's business, when we lived together in a spirit of friendship, and listened to our musician friends play their flutes and guitars so that the music was indistinguishable from the sounds of nature. When we would banter and consume many glasses of white wine with a meal of fish prepared for us by the grocer at the café where we would often meet in the evenings. That time of peace when we didn't have a single problem with the seagulls. Was there anyone who remembered any of this? You would've had to be blind not to see that the state of balance in which the island had existed was undone with the arrival of the President.

"I wouldn't want to turn out to be right, but in the belief that you'll carefully heed my following warnings, I want to emphasize once again that I am, in fact, right," the text continued. "If you continue to be led on by this man's crackpot ideas, we'll only be bound to encounter a new set of disasters.

And mark my words, all this business with the expert is also going to end in a fiasco. Then maybe you'll see that I was right, realizing how important it is that we unite against that man called the President and send him packing from this island."

The announcement ended with this audacious pronouncement: "I see this initiative as an opportunity, and as a test for me personally. Should the President turn out to be right in the days ahead, I'm prepared to take back everything I've said and to get on my knees and apologize before the President. If I should turn out to be right, however, let's please come to our senses and drive this man off the island for the sake of preventing any more of his madness and disaster."

After we'd finished handwriting copies of the announcement, the three of us each grabbed a stack of papers and distributed them to all the houses. But, of course, not to the President's nor to his armed men. We were sure it would reach the President nonetheless. Number 1 was certain to see to that.

One of the unforgettable events of that period was witnessing the heartbreaking tears of the grocer's son. When the boy showed up at the chicken coop one morning, he was met with horror: the chickens had been slaughtered. The foxes had dug a hole beneath the cage wire, leaving nothing alive. The place was strewn with the bodies of chickens that had been choked to death and left behind by the foxes after making off with the others. The boy's tears continued for days.

A week later, the feverish work of erecting a large group of pillars on the northern shore of the island had come to an end. All we had to do now was wait for the storks.

The same week, a neighbor or two who had been watching the horizon in anticipation of the ferry had noticed some birds in the far distance that they believed may have been storks. On hearing this news, we all gathered on the north shore of the island. We began to debate whether the approaching birds were storks or not. The expert, bringing his bony index fingers to his lips, signaled for us to be quiet. We all fell into a deep silence.

As the birds approached, we realized that they were indeed a flock of storks. The excitement on the island reached a palpable level as their expansive wings and slender torsos grew clearly distinguishable. The storks flew closer and closer, then alighted on the deserted island across from us. We could even sense the fatigue in the birds' wings, the closer they got to the island.

We looked at each other, baffled. Why hadn't they flown down onto the nests that had been prepared for them? everyone wondered. Would they come over here after resting on the other island for a while? A flurry of whispers spread among us. Perhaps it was the sight of the crowd of humans that was keeping the storks at bay, we surmised. So the crowd quietly dispersed, and all of us headed to the patch of pine trees at the top of the hill to watch events from there. The storks were walking around on the island across the way, drinking water, some of them scratching beneath their wings with their beaks. Then we watched them take flight once again. They rose up into the sky, flying directly above our island as we watched their every move. They circled around our island a few times, our eyes following in circles with them. We were all holding our breath. We were just about to get whiplash when, unfortunately, we saw the storks take off toward the south again. They flew off in one fell swoop as we stood looking on, crestfallen. We watched them until they disappeared on the southern horizon. At which point we had lost all hope. The shame that overcame us was so great that it became impossible to so much as look each other in the eye.

Someone asked where the expert was. At that point, everyone suddenly stirred to life, consumed with a burning desire to demand from the expert that he account for this course of events. But the expert was nowhere to be seen. We searched high and low, all the way to the pier.

The ferry had pulled up anchor. In the midst of watching the storks, we'd forgotten all about it, along with everything else.

It was the grocer who broke the bitter news: While we had been staring at the sky like fools, the expert had hopped aboard the motorboat and onto the ferry, which, as we could now see, had pulled up anchor and was quickly disappearing into the distance. When some of the islanders began to scold the poor grocer, the matter was instantly settled with his thoroughly reasonable reply: "How was I supposed to know that you wanted to stop the man?"

The expert was probably on deck counting his money as he thought about the people at the next stop who were awaiting the miracles he would work. In short, we had let him get away. We were to go on living on our cursed island, together with the poisonous snakes.

For most of us, our disappointment was so intense that we were in physical pain. Everyone was too distressed to speak in the days that followed, retreating into a corner and licking their wounds like animals. A few days later when people began to talk again, there was only one subject:

"I knew that guy wouldn't be able to achieve anything anyway!"

"So why didn't you say anything?"

"I don't know, the guy was just...so *tall*!"

"If it's size that matters, hell, camels are big, too!"

"Yeah, that's right! A camel is big and eats grass, but a falcon is small—and eats flesh!"

"What gullible fools we turned out to be!"

"Oh, come on, don't say that... Even if we hadn't believed him, what were we supposed to do?"

"You're right. Who else was there to believe?"

"Yeah! We don't have anyone to rescue us and show us the right way!"

"What was the President supposed to do, poor fellow. He has to deal with all kinds of problems all by himself."

"The people who are making problems for him and who are forever looking for opportunities to criticize him aren't giving it a rest, even in the midst of these days when unity is of utmost importance."

"No, no, the fact is, there's no telling what the President is going to say or do. He's unreliable."

"But he's the only one who's trying to find solutions, the only one trying to do something."

"You're right. Whenever there's a bad outcome, tongues start wagging."

Overhearing these exchanges was showing me that all my efforts to try to understand humankind were useless.

19

AFTER ALL THIS TIME and all the horrific events that have happened in the meantime, it's hard to believe that we'd talked only of literature on your last night on the island. But of course, there was no way for us to have known that it was your last night, my dear Writer. We believed that many such nights and days lay ahead of us.

That evening, you'd passed on to me the key wisdom on the art of narration: "Leave psychology, characterizations, and descriptions of human relationships out of it and just stick to describing what happens—the action," you'd said. "Don't go looking for prettier or more violent words to describe people. Just describe the action and let the reader fill in the rest in his head. This was Aristotle's advice, as well."

"'Why don't you give me an example," I said. You responded with this timeless parable of folklore:

"'There was once, in ancient times, a young man who fell in love with the daughter of a physician. She also was a dentist. The young man would visit the physician just so he could see the girl, and, as the rest of the story went, 'He had all thirty-two of his teeth pulled as he gazed upon the face of his beloved.' Now what other descriptions of love could you possibly add to that? They would all pale in comparison."

While we were having this conversation, as it later became clear, the President and his men were getting ready to deal their final blow against you. And in fact, it wasn't as though we didn't sense that the Shark felt the need to take some action, considering the compromised position he had found himself in on the heels of the stork fiasco and the expert's escape from the island. The President's authority on the island was crumbling, and he was having a hard time getting the people to believe in him now that they faced having to live with the snakes. There was no doubt he was planning a new operation, but the question was, how was he going to win the people over so that they would accept it?

I SPENT THAT NIGHT on pins and needles. That thing they call a premonition must really exist, I think. A person can sense ahead of time that something bad is about to happen. As I anxiously tossed and turned in bed, Lara asked me what was wrong. I said, "Nothing," but, knowing me as well as she did, she persisted. I told her of my fears. My heart was fluttering like a bird's. Lara revealed to me that she felt the same way. As it turned out, the two of us had been wrestling with similar dark premonitions.

After this disclosure, we sat outside in the yard, even managing to shrug off our fear of the snakes. Though we tried to comfort each other, it did no good. Our agitation was simply too great. The jasmines continued to give off their perfume at regular intervals in the meantime, but in our frame of mind, there was no comfort in them anymore. We had to figure out the future—that frightening and uncertain future of ours that loomed before us.

An announcement distributed to our houses the next morning informed us that we were to gather at the café early that evening. On receiving the flyer, we immediately realized that our premonitions of the night before had not been in vain, yet there was no way for us to have foreseen the events I'm about to describe.

T HE PRESIDENT introduced his speech by expressing his deep sorrow at the fact that everyone had been swindled at the hands of the expert. No one could be trusted in this day and age; morals had gone by the wayside. We'd seen as much with our own eyes; the very expert who had been recommended to him had turned out to be a fraud and run off without having found a single solution for dealing with the snakes. The President was ready to pay out of his own pocket for the damage incurred by the islanders, and so on. We listened to all of this without believing a word of it.

Then the President disclosed his new plan: since the snakes were still a problem, we were going to resort to the only solution left, which was to reduce the number of foxes on the island. Initially beneficial and of great service to the island, they had bred to excess and were now more harmful than beneficial. By reducing their numbers, and simultaneously raising the number of seagulls, it would be possible to reestablish nature's balance on the island and help solve the snake problem.

I squeezed Lara's hand. So then, the guns would reappear, and the once-calm islanders, each of whom had turned into a hunter in the meantime, would now be organizing a full-gear fox hunt.

After giving instructions for everyone to show up on the pier the next morning, the President said, "Now let's get to another matter. Dear friends, you'll recall that I made the choice to come to this island for reasons of security, and for the sake of being able to live in a secluded corner of the world far from terrorists after all the years of service I gave to my country."

A few people nodded a polite yes, to indicate that they did indeed recall the point. Lara and I were all ears, wondering what he was getting at.

"But unfortunately, dear friends," the President said, "I've failed to do this. The dangerous enemies of the country and of the regime have turned up before me here, too."

"What now?" we thought as we looked at each other. What was he getting at?

Just then, I heard Lara murmur, "No! It can't be..." I turned to look. The President's two men were bringing the Writer into the garden, bound in handcuffs. Immediately I shot up from my seat and made to go to him, but the President said, "Sit down in your seat. First listen to what I'm going to say, and then if you wish, you can go on.

"Recall if you will, dear friends, when we had our picture taken together. It was on one of the first days I came to your beautiful island. Well, those same pictures have been uploaded to the computers in our capitol and carefully investigated, exposing, as a result, the big secret of that friend of ours we so dubiously call the Writer. This person is a political convict who has escaped from prison, is an enemy of the regime, and has fooled you all by changing his name."

On hearing these words, everyone turned and looked at the Writer's face, but he went on boring his eyes into the President with a rancorous stare.

"Isn't that right, Mr. Writer?" asked the President. "Shall I go on to reveal what other special skills you possess, or have I said enough? Will you be the one to say that your wife was a subversive like you and committed suicide in jail, or shall I?"

An unspeakable pain shot through my heart. Clearly, the President was speaking the truth. This was the secret that lay behind the endless sad

expression in the Writer's eyes. Though unsophis-
ticated in these matters, even I knew that prison
suicides were a controversial issue. I had also
heard that opponents of the regime who had been
thrown in prison with no proof of having committed a crime, and for reasons unjustifiable even by
the regime's oppressive laws, would be reported as
having committed suicide, when the truth was that
they had been killed. And of course there were, in
fact, those who had actually committed suicide,
rather than choose the horrendous conditions under
which they would have had to live.

Lara dissolved into a flood of tears.

The President then stated that the Writer would
be held behind bars that night and taken away on
the motorboat the next morning, after which he
would be placed in the hands of justice.

The revelation had come as such a shock that
Lara and I sat there completely numb, unable to
move. I had no idea what to do in a situation like
this.

With his ever-present air of arrogance and pomp-
ous self-assurance, the President was saying appall-
ing things with his cruel, thin lips. He was asserting
that the Writer was the reason for the failures on our
island and ranting that social morale was extremely

important, as borne out by his personal service to the state, and that it was this very morale which the country's traitors most attacked.

Lara and I finally managed to gather our wits and stand up.

"We don't believe what you're saying," I said. "Our friend represents good on this island. You, on the other hand, represent evil. Everyone can bear witness to that fact. It isn't him but you who's brought this island to the state it's in. Until you came, this island was—"

Just then I felt a sharp pain at the back of my head, my eyes closed, and a wave of heat rose through my body. I have no recollection of what happened next. My head was throbbing when I opened my eyes. I was in an unfamiliar room. It must have been a room with no windows, something like a cellar. When I tried to force the door open, I found it locked. It wouldn't open.

According to what they told me later, the President's men struck the back of my head with the butt of a gun. Having knocked me unconscious, they dragged me off and locked me away in the President's cellar. Though they didn't hit Lara, they took her someplace where they also locked her up under police custody.

When they let us go the next day, the Writer had already been taken away on the motorboat. We never heard from him again.

N0, we never heard from you again, dear Writer. As you might imagine, all kinds of rumors cropped up in your absence. Calling me a traitor and Lara spineless, the neighbors now rushed in with all kinds of wild claims about you. They said you were a subversive to begin with, and said, with even greater conviction yet, that you were to blame for everything that had gone wrong on the island. In other words, my dear friend, you were responsible for everything that had happened. No one would believe us anymore because both Lara and I had been branded as untrustworthy for being friends of "the guilty one." Very few people still spoke with us.

All of this we endured, keeping our cool and gritting our teeth, but one day that patience came to an end and I punched a man in the face. Yes, *me*! I know how much you'd be surprised if you could read these lines; after all, how could someone like me *do* something like that?

But that man had been saying that after the motorboat had made it out to sea, they'd tied a heavy block of iron to your feet and tossed you overboard. What's more is that he'd said this with virtually no remorse, as if sharing the news of a good deed they'd done. One of the President's men had supposedly let it slip in the middle of conversation, after which the rumor evidently spread like wildfire.

Lara and I never believed a word of this. Even imagining you locked up in a prison back on the homeland was better than thinking of you as dead. Maybe someday, we would get on a boat and be free of this island, too; maybe we'd see you again, and talk to you again, and maybe you would even lay into me again on account of the way I've written this story.

Oh, my dear friend! Where are you? Where are you *really*?

So many rumors were sprouting up so quickly that it was as if the things we were hearing had begun to take the form of some kind of fable. You'd managed to escape from the hands of the President's men as they took you away on the motorboat, as one story had it—although unconvincingly. How could you have escaped when you were out there in the middle of the sea, your hands cuffed and a blindfold around your eyes?

Nonetheless, Lara and I couldn't help but wonder why a rumor like this should turn up. Maybe you really had escaped after all, but there was some mix-up in the details of the stories that were going around. Maybe instead of at sea, it had been once you were on land that you'd escaped. The President's men locked up your house and pronounced it off-limits. Luckily, they'd been somewhat slow to act. After making a visit to your place—in search of a keepsake, I presumed—Lara returned with a notebook in her hands, containing your notes. I must admit, I was surprised; I'd never seen you in the act of writing.

The notebook was indecipherable in parts, with one section set aside for what seemed to be the book you were going to write, though we were hard pressed to assign any significance to it. The notes in your journal, on the other hand, absolutely fascinated us. We realized that after going back home, you'd continued to give thought to what we'd talked about, having taken notes on the subjects in question, and on the unfolding developments in our lives.

Your sentences were all witnesses to the life of pain that you led, your thoughts enlightening, and my heart grieved as I read them. I remembered with gratitude your determination to live as a writer who preferred to take part within a noble and honorable movement rather than be a savior, and as someone who felt obliged to tell the truth as well as awaken others to it, willing to stand alone in doing so. I vowed that I would someday get your book published and read by the public.

So then, if I had to sum up what happened after you disappeared, it was a series of still more dreadful events.

The President and his men set off on a fox hunt that lasted for days. They would return swaggering early each evening, fox corpses in hand like so many trophies. As for the baby foxes, they would hook them on the notches on their belts. But kill and kill as they might, the foxes had proliferated to such an extent that they still couldn't kill them all. Besides which, it was impossible for them to check every rock cliff, and beneath every bush.

Following an accident in which one of the hunters shot one of his friends in the leg, the President/Shark and his men put their heads together with the islanders, having now turned them all into monsters, and decided to try out a brand-new method.

They had cyanide brought to the island. They were going to inject the dreadful poison into meat, which they would leave in the forest as a way to lure the foxes in their hunt. And indeed, that's exactly what they did, with devastating consequences. This time it wasn't only the foxes that were poisoned, but every species of creature that ate the meat. The island had become a death camp. The ground was so thick with the corpses of foxes, rabbits, partridges, turtles, sparrows, frogs, martens, and jackals that you had to step over them at every turn. The hunters were gathering up dozens of dead foxes a day and dumping them into a pile on the pier grounds, and still all this death wasn't enough for them. It was as if they'd come to breathe nothing but death, place their faith in nothing but death, talk of nothing but death. Were these people who, at this point, were suffering frightful bouts of hysteria on days they saw no blood the same calm, cheerful, and affectionate people we'd once known? Or was it that, little by little, we were losing our minds?

One day on my way to the pine forest, I saw a poisoned fox as it writhed in pain. It was tossing itself this way and that, no doubt from eating the poisoned meat. I doubt that I've ever witnessed anything more unbearable than this in my entire life.

The poor animal was twisting and turning around its big, bushy tail as though its flesh was being eaten alive. It had such an excruciating look of pain on its face—I couldn't even begin to describe it. It was as though the skin on its face was being stretched back, its teeth exposed because it couldn't close its mouth. Had I had a gun in my possession, I would have killed it on the spot to put it out of its misery. It suffered a long and painful death instead. The memory of it haunted me for days.

A few of our neighbors had fallen sick, as well. The doctor said it was because they'd ingested the poison. It appeared to us as though the President's face was also turning pale and taking on a decidedly yellowish hue. Some claimed that the animals that had been poisoned would go to the mouths of springs, only to die there and thus poison the island's spring water. Which was to say that we had all begun to drink water laced with cyanide.

Meanwhile, there was talk that you, dear Writer, had returned to the island and were hiding in the forest, scheming secret operations against the President, his men, and his followers. There were also suspicions that someone was helping you. The islanders' attitudes toward us began to grow stranger than ever.

Lara and I had begun to grow sickly, as well. It was high time we left the island, and really, we should have already left by then. We were waiting for the next ferry. We were going to get our stuff together and escape somewhere far away from this living hell of an island. In bed at night, I would twist and turn with questions for which I had no answer. So as not to disturb Lara, I would resist my urge to throw myself this way and that, thinking for hours on end instead, only to realize that she wasn't sleeping either, but was caught up in a maelstrom of dark thoughts of her own as she tried not to let on.

"Are you awake?" I would ask her. "Are you awake, sweetheart?"

Then we would step out into the garden and talk until dawn about where we would go, what city we would settle in, what we would do for a living. Lara would say that she could find a job as a waitress, or if worse came to worst, that she could work as a maid—neither of which sat right with me. After all those peaceful years on the island, the thought of returning to that other world chilled me, barbarous, merciless, and hideous as it was. Yet Lara was right; we couldn't go on living on that savage island anymore. What a shame it was for our secret paradise to have ended up this way. I would keep thinking of the same things and asking the same questions over and over again: Why didn't we have friends anymore? When we'd lived with them on the island like brothers and sisters, sharing days and nights with them, why had these people I'd once called angels turned into our enemies? These creatures weren't our islanders. A look of anger mixed with suspicion had settled into their eyes. They were no longer telling us of the decisions they were making.

When they saw that the cyanide was killing all the other creatures, I believe they did away with this measure, too, because, according to the buzz that was going around, the President was in hot pursuit of another idea.

The foxes could easily hide within the secluded corners of the forest, which was making it very difficult to shoot them. In order to force them out of their hiding spots, a controlled fire would be set in the forest. When the foxes ran out of the forest to escape the fire, they'd be finished off by the hunters lying in wait for them.

Since no one opposed the President, this plan was put into effect as well. A fire was set on one of the shores of the forest, sending off flames and plumes of smoke that we could see even though it was a good distance away from us. As the fire spread, the foxes and all the other creatures came running out and away as fast as lightning. It was difficult for the hunters to hit these swift animals. Still, they went on shooting at them with every effort they could muster, firing off one round after another. Lara was trembling as she covered her ears, rambling incoherently. It seemed to me that she was having a nervous breakdown.

The islanders had now focused the full brunt of their hatred onto the foxes, virtually forgetting the seagulls. And when the doctor said that the fox is the most contagious animal in the world, the fear and hatred among the islanders shot up even more, to the point they became something you could almost hold in your hands. He said that the cats and dogs that were bitten by foxes would catch their rabies and spread it to humans. As I listened, I wondered whether the rabies had already begun to spread on the island. Our islander friends were shooting with such enthusiasm and drunken rage that only rabid people could have shot that way.

The smell of soot reached our noses just then, as though wood were burning somewhere close by. Soon after, we saw smoke begin to fill the garden as shouts broke out here and there: "Fire! Fire! Everybody run!" It wasn't long before the heat of the approaching flames hit our faces.

My dearest friend, the islanders had so given themselves over to this shooting and killing spree that no one had noticed that what had begun as an offshore breeze was steadily building into a strong wind. Or rather, I should say, when they did, it was too late, and the forest fire had swallowed up everything in its path with the force of the violent wind.

It was as if the huge forest cried, shrieked, and exploded as it burned on. While the animals that were able to save their own lives came catapulting out of the forest like mad, there were also some who became coals among the flames.

The President's men and the islanders who had gone along with their ideas tried desperately to put out the fire, but we could all see that it would be impossible now. Our pine-nut trees crackled as they burst into flames, which spread to the trees on either side of the road that led from the pier, reaching the houses in the blink of an eye. If they had told me that a fire could spread this fast, I wouldn't have believed it, but sadly, that's exactly what happened. In no time, all the houses had caught fire, burning like dry kindling because they were made of wood. To escape the poisonous flames and plumes of smoke, we all ran off into the distance toward the seashore. When we turned to look at what we had left behind, we saw the giant trees as they virtually exploded into flames one after the other, like so many matchsticks struck along the fire's path.

With fear in their eyes, the islanders looked on, losing their minds to the terror that consumed them as the fire destroyed their houses one by one. There was nothing, absolutely nothing, that could be done.

20

THE SEAGULLS were flying above us as though they were mocking us all, watching this burnt, bleak island and its people who no longer had so much as a shred of shelter. Had they attacked at that moment, there would have been nothing we could have done to stop them. But they didn't attack us. Instead they made do with simply flying above us. With no damage done to their shore, they could go on breeding, hunting, and watching over their eggs with a sense of security just as before. In short, they'd won this war.

As for us losers, we were sleeping out in the open, and fishing, thanks to the rowboat that had remained intact, as we waited for our rescue. By that I mean the ferry that we fervently hoped was going to take us away from here.

The day after the fire, we gathered at the edge of the cliff to take in the damage that had been done. Being the highest point over the island, it afforded the best vantage point. It was none other than the spot from which the grocer's son had released the seagull chicks into their first flight. Standing with our neighbors as tears welled up in their eyes, we saw the full extent of the disaster. Black plumes of smoke were wafting into the sky. The smell of the fire's destruction permeated the air. Everything had burned down, including the cemetery where we buried our dead.

Though it didn't sound at all credible to me, talk of the Writer dying while hiding in the burning forest angered me in the extreme. Not because it meant that the friend I loved so much had died, but because it meant that we no longer had any hope.

And in any case, those who disagreed that the Writer had died in the forest would point out that he'd been thrown into the sea with a block of iron tied to his feet. I believed neither of these rumors. I really didn't know what to believe. Some time later, the President and his men showed up, likewise surveying the island. Then the President made a speech in which he informed us that he was about to leave the island on the motorboat, never to set foot here again. He had issued all the necessary instructions, there was no need to fear, and the ferry that would collect us was already on its way.

I noticed that he didn't say a word about the disaster he'd caused, and that he showed no sign of guilt. He was talking like a stranger who had nothing to do with any of these matters. In fact, it seemed that he even expected us to thank him for going to the trouble of rescuing us from the island.

Lara began to speak.

"Are you leaving now, Mr. President?"

"Yes, in just a few minutes!"

"How unfortunate that you should leave defeated."

"What do you mean, 'defeated'?"

"Yes, Mr. President, I spoke quite clearly: you've been defeated."

"And just who has defeated me, young lady?" the President asked in an angry tone.

"The seagulls!" answered Lara. "Just raise your head and take a look around. They're making fun of you as they fly in the sky and send you packing."

And indeed, the seagulls were flying about both overhead and in the abyss of the precipice as the President stood at its edge.

Upon hearing her words, he began to shout: "You boor! Is it for a young woman to talk to her elder this way? How could the seagulls possibly have defeated me! Everything that's happened to you has been the result of your ineptitude and siding with anarchists like that embarrassment of a Writer. I'm leaving, to hell with all of you. This island doesn't concern me anymore."

When they heard this, the island community grumbled and scowled at the President for the first time.

"You can see for yourselves," I said. "The disaster is before your very eyes. He's the man responsible for everything. It was this man who destroyed our island."

A few people in the crowd groused, "You're right. Everything was going just fine up until this man got here."

"If only you'd never set your damned feet on this island!" the notary shouted. Seeing the situation take a turn for the worse, the President panicked. He tried to turn the argument onto Lara again.

"You've become inhuman, young lady" he said. "Even when people are fighting for their lives, you engage in provocation for the sake of your own political aims. I've dealt with subversives like you my entire life. I know your kind inside and out. And the likes of you and your husband deserve to end up in the same place as that traitorous Writer friend of yours. Besides, all the decisions made on this island were carried out democratically. We carried out whatever the majority vote resulted in. As a result, all the decisions bore everyone's signatures beneath them—and I just dare any one of you to come out and say I'm wrong about that. Come on! I dare you!"

Something came over me just then. Feeling a wave of heat rising up into my head and my heart beating like a drum, I spoke, in a voice choked with rage: "*I* say you're wrong, Mr. Shark! *I* say you're wrong! *I* say you're wrong, you cruelest of the cruel! Now that you've destroyed everything, don't you dare go trying to tell us any of your half-baked tales of democracy!"

Had I not been so irate, had my cheeks and ears not been burning so furiously, the look of shock on the President's face may well have made me laugh.

Meanwhile, complete silence had fallen over the neighbors as they looked on in astonishment, for the first time in their lives witnessing their friends show anger, raise their voices, and express their opposition. I was overcome with a rush of rebellion, ready even to risk death. My head was swimming. What had gotten into me?

"That's enough!" the President said, raising his hand. "You will stop talking this very instant, or I'll make you regret the day your mother bore you!"

We knew him well by now. We were familiar with the threat conveyed in his voice, as it would grow high-pitched whenever he got angry.

Lara stepped in front of me. "What more harm could you possibly do?" she said. "What more harm could you possibly do?" I repeated, stepping in front of her this time. At that moment, however, it occurred to me what terrible things the President could do to Lara. It was a thought that didn't merely scare me—it terrified me. There was nothing I wanted now but for Lara to be quiet and to be free of this senselessness. It wouldn't have mattered one bit what happened to me, but if they were to lay so much as a finger on Lara, I could have gone berserk. That boldness I'd felt had now left me, in its place a fear so intense I shivered.

Then he turned and issued an order to his men. "Place these two traitors under arrest for insulting the President and starting an insurrection. They're coming with us."

The men with the dark glasses approached us, taking Lara by the arm before seizing me in their grip. I looked at my neighbors in desperation. Were they going to allow them to take us away like this after all those rumors of the Writer being thrown in the sea with a block of iron tied to his feet? Were our friends of all these years going to abandon us? They might have been able to save us if they'd only put up a little objection. Yet I was unable to meet any of their eyes. They'd all looked away.

But at that very moment, something happened: it was both the most mournful and most courageous deed I've witnessed in my entire life.

With a scream that frightened even the seagulls, and the first we were hearing his voice, the grocer's hunchbacked son ran at full speed toward the President and hit him, the force of the collision sending them both tumbling off the face of the cliff. We saw the two bodies flailing as they fell through the void and struck the ground, where they smashed to pieces. Being the heavier of the two, the President had struck the ground slightly before the grocer's son.

Petrified, we looked down from the top of the cliff.

The grocer's mute son had attacked just like the suicide-bombing seagulls, but with far greater results. As I remembered the way we had released the fledglings from the edge of this cliff not all that long ago, tears burst from my eyes. I could still see those wobbly chicks, learning to fly as they skipped from one rock mass to another.

This was the first time we were hearing the voice of this disabled boy whom no one had noticed, nor treated like a human being, yet I doubt that those who had heard his scream would ever be able to forget it. It was a scream full of anger and protest; an astounding scream let out against all the injustice and evil in the world.

And then the heartrending screams of the grocer and his wife rang out, shaking the earth and sky.

The President's camp took off in a flash, jumping on the motorboat as they sped away. We were left on the island a small crowd, wounded, hurt, grief-stricken, and enraged. Up until the next day, when the military units came and collected us all and transferred us to the famous prison in the capitol.

The military ship sat like a castle on the surface of the sea as its assault boats convoyed us from the pier. Clad in starched khaki uniforms, bearing stony expressions hewn across their faces with all the delicacy of a battle-ax, the soldiers locked us up in chains once we boarded the ship.

The President's body parts were gathered up from the rock masses onto which they'd fallen and brought aboard with a ceremony. The soldiers and officers were looking at us with such mortal hatred that we were doing everything in our means not to meet eyes with them. Because they were separating the men from the women, I couldn't see Lara. My right hand had been handcuffed to Number 1. We didn't talk to each other, but his sunken shoulders and the look in his eyes, like that of a beaten dog, revealed a deep sense of remorse. Having ignored the warnings they had been given at every turn, the neighbors who had once embraced the President were now locked up no differently than we were.

Yet, what dreams they had harbored for the island. We would become rich, we would live in affluence and ease, and we would live in freedom on the island. In the end, everyone had lost: the President, those who had followed him, and those who had challenged him. There was no winner. Perhaps, as Lara had said, all except for the seagulls, who would be left in peace from now on. We had been defeated for having submitted, and for not having seen how much worse the evil we'd been dragged into could get. We should have started speaking out and rebelling back when the trees were pared away and the grocer's innocent son was beaten. We had accepted the President's every step with the utmost naivete. The seagulls had won because they had taken a stand and fought instead of compromising. That being the case, wouldn't we be wise to ask who was the more intelligent—the people who submitted, or the seagulls who rebelled?

So then, we're here in the cells for now. They've been badgering us with questions in attempts to find out who planned this operation.

I've been writing these lines from inside my dank and murky cell, my hands aching.

I don't hear from Lara, and have no way of knowing what may have happened to her. Nor do I know whether the Writer is in the same prison. I know nothing, absolutely nothing.

I only know that there's a strange rumor going around. In the cafeteria, in the laundry room, or on the way to being interrogated, there are whispers to the effect that the Writer is still on the loose. Apparently, some have seen him, as he was on his way back to the island. They say he's going to start living there again these days. That he's going to plant new trees. Build new homes. And that some of his old friends are going to go help him. The island's going to come back to life, they say. We're going to live on the island again. We're going to reestablish our paradise on earth.

I try not to think of that last wounded look Lara shot me when they separated us on our way off the boat. I may go mad if I do. I may go insane, smashing my head to bits as I bang it on my cell walls. So, I've blocked out my thoughts. I've made myself numb.

They said that the President's funeral was carried out with a big state ceremony that aired live on TV, and that after wrapping the ebony coffin containing the President's broken body in a flag, they loaded it onto a gun carriage. Moreover, they said, speeches were made that praised the President's heroism and the sacrifices he had so courageously made on behalf of his country; condemned the terrorists committed to bringing the country down; and even condemned the head terrorist himself, the grocer's son. After which the President was buried in the cemetery of heroes, amid the tears of his family and the nation.

Here's where the memories end. And now there's nothing left to distract me from the questions that riddle my mind, day in and day out: "My love, where are you? Where are you? Where?"

My dear friend; noting the advice that the Istanbul gardener gave to Candide in that book by Voltaire: "Grow your garden," you once had said to me. "Tell your story!" Do you remember? "Just tell your story!"

And that is what I've done.

EPILOGUE

The sea was choppy that day, and we clung to the old fishing boat's railing, which shook like a nut in its shell. We were tired from the hours of waves and strong winds, the odor of fish permeating the wood, the overly loud engine noise, but all this was nothing compared to our heart-pounding excitement. As we drew closer, we strained to see the island, shielding our eyes from the hot sun. The island, our island, that ruined paradise. We pictured it from indelible memories of eleven years ago. In our prison cells, during our long persecution, we tried most of all to recapture that happiness, reliving the scent of jasmine on our skin.

Lara had been in a women's prison, so I was unable to see her for years, but within prison life there is a secret web of human relationships that defy the rules, whether out of self-interest, solidarity, or pity. Thanks to that network, I learned that Lara was in good health. I will never know what her existence looked like then, but she was probably waiting in a facility with the same harsh conditions as ours.

What were we waiting for? I have to say: nothing. The country's harsh laws and harsher judges, who scrutinize defendants with hatred throughout their trials, had condemned us to life imprisonment. Only our corpses would leave these thick, damned walls. Knowing this makes you despair, and prevents any dreams or plans. The press no longer talked about us. As vigilante terrorists, we were forgotten in dank, dark cells. I drew a seagull on the damp wall of mine with the handle of a spoon. A huge seagull, free and fearless, with its wings spread wide. I spent my days looking at it and thinking about what it means to rebel, to not bow down to oppression, to resist. People who don't resist oppression lose their dignity and self-respect. The sly, dirty expression of a collaborator settles on their faces. We had seen it with our own eyes in our neighbors.

L ara was sitting at the front of the boat, as if that would bring her to the island a few meters sooner. I was with her, one hand holding on to her slender shoulder. The foamy white waves that rocked the boat sprinkled saltwater on our faces, sometimes soaking us from head to toe. Well, after being in the dark like nocturnal insects for all these years, it was as though rediscovering the exhilaration of nature and the vast sea was washing our souls, too.

Lara suddenly cried out, "Look, look!" She pointed at a seagull circling in the air. Ah, those seagulls, our seagulls, our rebellious friends who don't bow down to oppression. Seeing that seagull filled us with the joy of life, and we knew we were nearly there. Soon we would glimpse that injured island, that wonder again. Whether it burns or collapses, it's our island, our home.

I t shouldn't be hard to imagine what it was like that day, when the guard opened the iron door with a bang and told us we were free, while we had been waiting, hopeless, for death to come after an age in that blind darkness. Disbelief, doubt, sudden sweat, dizziness, knees buckling. But eventually it all passed, and that day we learned that states shift over time according to the gangs who lead them. As we were languishing there, a coup had taken place: the government, the sharks, were captured by the President's opponents, and they issued a general amnesty. I think they put supporters of the old regime in our cells instead, but we didn't care about that. We understood the rules of the game now: one was coming, the other going, but nothing changed. The game has always been the same.

T he seagulls started to multiply, circling above our heads, gliding gracefully across the sky with their white wings. Our seagulls must have died; maybe these were hatchlings from the eggs we tried to protect, and maybe their offspring, too.

Then our island appeared indistinctly on the horizon. Lara and I hugged each other. Our hearts beat in our ears. As we approached, the island grew and grew and grew; we could make out burned trees. For years we had dreamed hopelessly to just see our island again. Here it was before us. The color of the water began to change, taking on a dazzling shade between pale blue and turquoise. The waves subsided, and silverback fish were visible in the aquarium-like sea. We felt as though we had been cast out of heaven but come back again. Lara was crying tears of happiness. As we got closer, we discovered something else. The trees were black, but the ground was green with all kinds of wild plants. Nature, which humans had harmed so much, was regathering itself, preparing to sing again with its trees, plants, birds, and bugs.

Since there was no pier where it could dock, the fishing boat left us in water that came to our chests, and we carried our tent, food, and clothes to land by going back and forth between the boat and the shore. We thanked the kindhearted fisherman who had brought us here for only fuel money and said goodbye until we would see him next week. Then we sat on the shore waving as we watched the blue-green fishing boat disappear into the distance.

As we walked toward the tree line to set up our tent, we were startled by a male voice calling "Welcome!" My heart leapt to say "Writer" before I even saw the man. But it wasn't him. Two men and three women were approaching us from the depths of the forest. We had never expected this.

We were astonished and couldn't understand how these young people came to be here. They shook our hands, offered us water from a flask, and then asked who we were. It was their turn to get excited when we said we were two of the original inhabitants of the island. They hadn't heard we had been released from prison, so it was hard to believe they had suddenly come across us on the island. Then we asked them who they were. They said, we will tell you, but rest first. They gathered our things and took us into the scorched forest. As we entered, we saw that some trees were quite green, and the green plants covering the ground provided coolness and moisture, even though there was little shade. We admired how nature repairs itself, but our next sight a little farther on would increase our joy a thousandfold: Our house was in front of us. It was the same house, with its veranda, roof, doors, windows. Lara and I looked at each other. How was this possible? Were we dreaming?

A girl brought cold water and sat us on the veranda before telling us everything we were curious to know. We were amazed as we listened, and listened as we were amazed. Apparently, while we were being tried for the crime of killing the dictator, the case was written about daily in the country's papers and reported on television. Our pictures were featured. They said we had established an indecent, illegal, immoral way of life on the island, and that when the state intervened, we killed the President and set the island on fire. Of course, they convinced a majority of the people, who were under the influence of the press. Everyone was cursing us, except for some of the youth. They never believed what they were told, because they knew there was a game behind every news story the government and the press spread. They searched for the truth for a long time, and this led them to see us as heroes and legends, especially Lara and the grocer's son, who even appeared on posters with revolutionary slogans. Finally, as a volunteer movement, they decided to make the island green again, and turn it into a symbol of freedom and resistance. Nine friends came here and built this house according to a plan they drew from some of the half-burned houses. As before, they arranged stones and planted jasmine, geraniums, and saplings around it, and the saplings had already started to grow.

This small scene affected us so deeply after the long years in prison and so much sadness and anxiety that Lara, tough as she was, had tears in her eyes. It was like a dream; we couldn't believe it.

The young people were staring at us with admiration, without believing it. They even apologized for not recognizing us at first. Seagulls were circling in the sky, the sea was taking on the delicious colors of the sunset, from dark blue to purple, purple to pink, and the beautiful scents in the gentle breeze were reinvigorating us. Yes, we believed now. We were going to rebuild our island. The dictator who had done so much damage had lost.

There was only one question left. We were afraid of the answer but needed to ask.

"The Writer," I said. "Have you seen him?"

After such good news, I had an unrealistic hope.

Lara was staring straight ahead.

The young people looked at each other for a while without speaking. Then a long-haired girl said, "Every revolution demands sacrifices," and fell silent.

We asked nothing more.

THE LAST ISLAND
DISCUSSION QUESTIONS

1. Most characters in the novel are named for a singular attribute: their house number or their profession. What is the significance of this? Why do you think Lara is called by her given name?

2. How does the writer-narrator of the novel relate to the character known as "the Writer"? What do these two representations—the writer as passive observer vs. the writer as active/activist—say about the power (or the impotence) of writing?

3. On page 181, the narrator thinks to himself, "So. This is [the President's] nature then—the nature of

a shark." Discuss the use of animal metaphors in the novel. What do these metaphors suggest about the relationship between a person's "nature" and personal responsibility? How are different characters either excused or held accountable for actions arising from their "nature"? What animal would you use to describe your nature?

4. Discuss the increasingly violent encounters between the islanders and the seagulls. Is a provoked minority culpable for a violent reaction to a clear aggression?

5. Which character's response and perspective do you most identify with? What would your reaction be if you were a resident of the Island?

6. What does the novel suggest about the possibility of utopia? Do you think it's possible to create an ideal society, or will any attempt inevitably be corrupted?

7. What does the epilogue suggest about the transmission of culture and ideology from generation to generation? In what ways are these traditions ruptured? In what ways are they perpetuated?

Q&A WITH AUTHOR ZÜLFÜ LIVANELI ON *THE LAST ISLAND*

Q: The narrator of *The Last Island* nicknames this place "Isle of Angels" (4). What he describes is almost a utopia: "Everyone simply did as much as they could, or felt like doing" (119). This doesn't last long, however, and what begins in the novel as a utopia turns into a complete dystopia. If we extrapolate the Island to the Earth, do you think this is universal and inevitable?

ZL: *The Last Island* is perhaps my most political novel, although it doesn't describe a particular country. I preferred to write what I think about Turkey and the world through the lens of people living on a remote island, seagulls, and a dictator. Because I thought that

I could tell the truth—which has been lost and over-looked among millions of news details—more easily by isolating it. People find it difficult to distinguish truth from falsehood when they're being bombarded with targeted news. In any case, large groups of people forget the past; they don't think about the future, they only live in the moment. This "moment" is often misinterpreted, as it is shaped by the manipulations of governments and the media.

Q: In the novel, the President begins to save the island society from "anarchy" by ordering the trees on the wooded path "pruned, cleared out, and fixed up in keeping with park and garden traditions" (48), which brings to mind common misconceptions of green space by local governments and the events of Gezi Park, albeit indirectly. Once again life seems to imitate art! As a writer and artist known to be mindful of the environment, what would you say?

ZL: I've become more and more convinced that life imitates art. Indeed, *The Last Island*, which was published years before the Gezi resistance, seems to overlap with it. So when you manage to look at life accurately, you can pass into a dimension outside of time and space through art. World and Turkish literature are full of many similar examples. It is the job of journalism to relate the events of Gezi immediately, sociology to interpret them after the fact, and art to represent them with predictions informed by history.

Q: The President starts to rule the Island with the help of "committees." This development doesn't attract much attention at first, and gives no hint as to how serious things would turn out to be: "it was all theater, nothing more" (63). Every fascist government's future victims watch its first acts as they would a game. Can we say that these performances are still staged today?

ZL: Every dictatorship is careful, in the beginning, to present its own interest as the interest of society. It tries not to scare anyone. Then, as its strength and confidence grow, it gradually starts to show its teeth. Of course, this characterization is valid not for violent upheavals like the French Revolution, but for "elected kings" who rise to power through supposedly "democratic" means.

Q: One of the novel's most important messages is that fascism may well be a majority power that takes hold through democratic means. Connected to this is the fact that democracy can actually be a deceptive concept, with very painful consequences: "all the decisions made on this island were carried out democratically. We carried out whatever the majority vote resulted in" (283). A familiar voice right here [in Turkey] says, "The majority is right!" So, what do you think?

ZL: In the seventies, the *Cumhuriyet* newspaper conducted interviews with the condition that responses must be brief. In one such interview, I defined democracy as "dictatorship of the majority," and this concept generated a lot of discussion. At that time, the word "democracy" was highly exalted, and many people didn't like my definition. However, this is how the French sociologist Maurice Duverger defines democracy. Of course, this definition describes a cruel game played behind a mask, and not true, ideal democracy. For a regime to be democratic in the full sense of the word, it must be based on pluralism, not the majority, and it must fully implement the separation of powers. Now these concepts have become better understood with the painful experiences we're living. For example, who can control the government in a regime where the judiciary has become pathetic!

Q: The dictator's dilemma is that he undermines himself with the repressive methods he uses to maintain

his rule—unintentionally, of course, or almost unintentionally, with an "armed propaganda" approach:
"What was happening to us had taken us by such
surprise that we couldn't think straight. But we were
well aware of one thing: it never occurred to us to be
angry with the seagulls. On the contrary, the hatred
we felt toward the President had only increased for
causing all of this in the first place" (174). Did you
dwell on this connection while writing?

ZL: The power game inevitably results in the players
being poisoned by power. Dictators make the mistake of assuming they can "set the course" by relying
on the armed people under their command. History,
however, is full of examples that show this isn't possible. Every dictator—like Mussolini—is hung by his
feet, continues to struggle until this symbolic hanging. While I was writing the novel, I had military
dictatorships and the Kurdish question (seagulls) in
mind, but later on, other connections emerged. It was
strange, as though someone who has read the novel
were trying to apply it to the real world.

Q: The novel ends with hope for the future in a dark
place where everyone has lost except the seagulls,
who won "because they had taken a stand and fought

instead of compromising," and the narrator laments, "We should have started speaking out and rebelling back when the trees were pared away and the grocer's innocent son was beaten" (288). As the Writer says, "wherever there's evil, everyone there is partly to blame for it" (168). Now that we've started to talk about the "Gezi Spirit," has your hope increased a little bit?

ZL: I agree with these statements. Anyone who doesn't stand up to evil as it looms becomes part of the crime. It's necessary to say no to dictatorships that "slowly" gain ground. Rebels are noble for that. Yes, the seagulls win because they resist. The novel focuses on the fact that society and nature will find, or rather must find, their balance. If you try to interfere with these balances, the result is disastrous; both nature and human beings are destroyed. This murder is sometimes committed openly in the form of a dictatorship, sometimes hidden behind the deception of "democracy"—the will of a single person, boards, assemblies, commissions, etc. But they're all distractions. Decisions come from one person. That one person, however, degenerates over time with power, beginning to believe that God created him to rule the world, and trying to dominate nature and society. He even sees this as his most natural right, gets angry—genuinely angry—with those who oppose it. He interprets society raising its voice as "the feet becoming the head." Honestly, I was more hopeless while writing the novel, but the Gezi resistance blew my mind, as it did many others'. This unorganized, spontaneous movement seemed to me to be proof that humankind is inexhaustible. I'm glad to have had the chance to live through those historic days together with young friends. By adding an epilogue to the novel, I wanted to send a salute to the resisting youth.

ZÜLFÜ LIVANELI is Turkey's best-selling author and a political activist. Widely considered one of the most important Turkish cultural figures of our time, he is known for his novels that interweave diverse social and historical backgrounds, figures, and incidents, including the critically acclaimed *Bliss* (winner of the Barnes & Noble Discover Great New Writers Award), *Serenade for Nadia* (Other Press, 2020), *Disquiet* (Other Press, 2021), *Leyla's House*, and *My Brother's Story*, which have been translated into thirty-seven languages, won numerous international literary prizes, and been turned into movies, stage plays, and operas.

AYŞE A. ŞAHIN is a Turkish-American translator and bilingual language educator based in Istanbul. To learn more about her work, visit ayseaydansahin.com.